JAMIE'S ROCK

JAMIE'S ROCK

A STORY OF TIBET

L. GARY GOLDMAN

The characters and events in this novel are mostly fictional as are some of the locations, such as *Gönpoy-Ri*. The political turmoil and human rights abuses as depicted in Tibet are based on just a few of many like events that have occurred in that amazing but tragic country. Novels need villains and heroes. Most in this novel are invented although I have met variations of both in my life.

Cover art by China Adams (www.chinaadamsart.com)

Author photo courtesy of Louis Kravitz (www.louiskravitz.com)

ISBN-13: 978-0-6157-3637-2

Burning Synapse Press
POB 480857
Los Angeles, CA 90048

There are few events as tragic as the history of modern Tibet. This novel is dedicated to its long suffering people: May you and your magnificent wisdom culture soon be free to once again carry on your lives and traditions for the benefit of all beings...

... and to Griffin, my best friend and muse, who was either patiently right next to me through all of this writing or sleeping on my lap. I so miss you, old friend.

"When your bones grow weary, come live inside my heart,
there's room enough for both of us.
Lay your body down, live inside my heart,
there's room enough for both of us.
(Artimis Robison, 2012)

Chapter 1

DISCOVERY

NEW YORK CITY, JANUARY 12

Angela silently stares at the screen... *jet lag is killing me... stay awake, at least <u>pretend</u> you're paying attention ... God, is Marty looking at me again?... what's up with him?... can't believe that Emily was ever interested in him... has to be half his age... <u>focus</u>!... sleep on the plane... got to call Jamie, tell him I'll be home tonight... NOW what's he done? —*

The screen goes dark. Angela squints as the lights come up... *and here we go...*

She glances around... *got to be a million dollar room... that screen and the seating alone is —*

The clapping startles her. Marty and Emily, both wearing that particularly ubiquitous sign of Corporate America, the enhanced security ID card, held for all to see by a gold neck strap emblazoned with "Cable Broadcast News" (although Emily has hers looped around her wrist), clap appreciatively as Angela appreciatively smiles ... *that neck strap really clashes with her jacket... bet that's why she wears it on her wrist...*

Marty gives two thumbs up, flashing a killer smile along with a tastefully tailored French cuff. "Wow, and I really mean that."

Angela mutters, "Thank you" as she thinks... *is he one of those people who has memorized what a big smile feels like and can slap it on anytime he likes?...*

Emily enthusiastically turns in her seat toward Angela. "This is wonderful, Angela! Powerful! When will it be ready?"

... never 'cause I'll be screwing with it until someone finally buys it... "In a couple of months."

"That long? Two months?"

"I'm going back for interviews and shots I couldn't get on the first trip."

Emily looks at her notebook, then at Marty. "We should schedule an air date now anyway."

"I concur." He smiles at Angela. "You've got that same great eye Jake had."

Emily shoots Marty a "now you've done it" look. He shakes his head. "Christ, sorry, I'm usually not this dumb."

"It's okay." *… it's not okay… you knew about Jake…*

Emily cuts in, "We'll get the deal memo to your agent a-s-a-p."

Angela glances at her watch as she gathers her things. "Great, thanks. Look, I hate to run but I've got a plane to catch."

Marty looks physically hurt. "You're leaving? Now? I thought we could all pop out to dinner at least."

"Can I get a rain check? I'm just buried in LA."

There's that huge smile again. "Of course. Next time, for sure, promise?"

"Promise." They all stand and walk to the door.

Emily takes her by the arm, "How's that son of yours? He's some kind of a genius as I recall."

Angela rolls her eyes. "Mostly, he's a teenager. You have any idea what that means?"

LOS ANGELES

It's a typical scene for LA and most big American cities. A mixed group of teen-aged boys and girls, dressed in the most fashionable wannabe gangbanger/vampire/Goth attire, their hair done up from artfully tattooed skulls to the colorfully fanciful to the just plain sloppy, is clustered around a more conventionally attired boy... at least his pants are pulled up somewhere in the vicinity of his hips. Jamie Edwards isn't cringing, but he's getting flashes that maybe he ought to be somewhere else. Right. But actually, in some adolescently near self-destructive way, not really. This is the big time.

In that cool and casual way that demands many hours of practice, they sign, bang and tap and grab fists in carefully choreographed greetings that say far more about stylistic importance than the actual greeting itself, when a simple "Hey, how's it going?" would suffice for simply informational purposes.

Jamie carefully watches, ... *chill... don't be a dork... you can do this...* makes eye contact for just a moment with a pretty but weirdly dressed girl, trying his best to maintain his own cool, maybe some detached aloofness, above all of this childish posturing without looking too much like an idiot but hell, something's still causing sweat to run down his back.

Then the group leader, Slammer, an alpha male if ever there was one, with that perfect sense of style precisely married to an unspoken dangerous physicality abruptly turns and gets right into Jamie's face and softly whispers, "Jamie. You're the nerd-bitch."

"Screw you. Its just Jamie." More flop sweat.

Slammer's eyes never leave Jamie's... *damn... thought this cracker was s'posed to have some brains...* "Ooo... okay, 'Just-Jamie'."

He laughs, quite pleased with his own cleverness, then shouts out to the rest of his crew as his eyes stay in Jamie's.

"Yo! 'Just-Jamie' gots somethin' to show us." His crew laughs appreciatively. "Lessee what'cha got." Slammer points to a parked Lexus. "That's shithead Jackson's car." Slammer saunters over to the car and a switchblade knife suddenly appears in his hand. His knees barely bend as the knife slams into the sidewall of the front tire. The air HISSES out and the car leans to one side.

"There. Okay, it ain't goin' nowhere. Now do it." He shrugs. "Or don't do it. Don't make a shit to me."

Jamie pulls a can of spray paint out of his bag. He pops off the cap and pauses.

"S'amatter, 'Just-Jamie'? Gonna punk out on me?"

"I can do it." Jamie begins to spray a tag on the car. As the "letters" appear, there's something not quite right—they are very different from the "normal" tags... almost foreign. Slammer cocks a quizzical eye. "The fuck kinda tag izzat?"

"Huh?"

"Damn, 'Just-Jamie', didn't your daddy teach you nothin'?"

Jamie's face suddenly hardens. "He didn't have time. He's dead."

Slammer stares into Jamie's eyes with a new found appreciation for this slightly weird kid. "Now who woulda guessed? We got somethin' in common."

Just then, another kid runs toward Slammer. "Hey! Freakin' guard's coming!"

It's as if a bomb went off—kids scatter in all directions leaving Jamie alone. A look of panic crosses his face and he drops the can of paint with a CLANG, turns to run, and crashes smack into one of those shaved-head, Oakley-glassed school security guards all dressed in black with boots and a harness as if he was on one of the LAPD's kick-in-the-door SWAT teams.

"Gotcha'! Boy, old man Jackson's gonna hand you your young ass on a plate!" Jamie's face is wild with fear, and then a crashing sense of resignation sinks in as he's led off toward the school.

. . .

Principal Jackson sits behind his carefully organized desk. He's one of those principals who looks as if he might have been a football coach at one time—close-cropped hair, big forearms—one with a Marine globe and anchor tattoo, big hands, shirt-sleeves rolled up to the elbow, tie loosened a bit as he peers through incongruous maroon granny glasses at a file folder. He makes a few notes with his pen, closes the folder and reaches for another. He glances up at Jamie for a moment... *yeah, good, just sit there, kid... sweat a little...*

He peers over his glasses, but his face is expressionless as his eyes return to the folder on his desk. Even so, it's an intimidating look and Jamie defensively slouches down.

...I am so screwed... Jamie glances over at his grandfather, Ed, early 60s, closely cropped grey hair, kind of a hard looking man who glances at his watch and silently shakes his head. Jamie squeezes his eyes together for a moment. *... I am so totally screwed...* His shoulders slump as he uncomfortably sits back in his chair.

Suddenly, the door to the office opens and Angela breathlessly enters. "I'm so sorry. My plane was late. I came straight here."

Principal Jackson looks up, removes his glasses and motions to an empty chair next to Jamie. "Please, take a seat Mrs. Edwards. Can I get you something to drink?"

. . .

The three adults silently regard Jamie. When the boy speaks, his voice is almost a whisper.

"Sorry, Mr. Jackson."

Jackson curiously looks at Jamie. "What were you thinking?"

Jamie's eyes rest on the desk. "I don't know."

Jackson dials it up a bit. "Look at me when I speak to you."

Jamie raises his eyes and tries to meet Jackson's.

"Why'd you do it?"

Jamie's at a loss. He shrugs his shoulders.

Jackson shakes his head, "I don't get it. Why do you even hang out with that crowd?"

Jamie's eyes are focused on the desk again as he shrugs. "They're kinda cool."

"Cool, huh? I hate to say this about any young person, but those kids are losers... all of this swagger crap. If they're really lucky, barring the likelihood of a major run-in with law enforcement or some kind of drug-induced coma, maybe they'll be flipping burgers some day when their families cut them off. Now you, I don't know what to think. You're one of the most gifted students we've ever had. Your astronomy projects are world class, and here you are, about to flush what could be an incredibly marvelous future right down the toilet. You need to take a hard look at yourself, young man. Get a grip before you lose it all. Use that brainpower to dig your way out of the hole you're falling into. Now, I want to talk with your mother and grandfather in private. Close the door behind you and wait until we're done."

Jamie awkwardly stands, unable to look at either his mother or his grandfather and silently exits the office.

Angela reaches for her purse as she speaks. "Mr. Jackson, I'll take care of the damage right away— " She's interrupted by the principal.

"It <u>kills</u> me to see an immensely talented young person like Jamie, with all the promise that he has, consciously decide to throw it all away just so he can fit in with what will probably be the future inmates of our prison system. It worries me that you haven't been here for the last two parents meetings—"

Ed almost comes out of his seat, "Shit in your hat and squeeze it, Mister! I was there! And you've got some punk-assed kids—"

Angela turns to him, "Ed, please!"

Jackson holds a hand up as he speaks. "I don't meant to infer that no one cares about Jamie, but Mrs. Edwards, you are his mother and—"

Angela is almost in tears. "Jamie's father is dead. I'm doing everything I can to see that we can afford to send him to the best schools and that means that I have to be gone a lot. It breaks my heart that I can't be with him more."

She pauses to wipe her eyes. "I'm supposed to leave for India and Tibet next week. I'll cancel the trip." She takes a moment to wipe her eyes.

Jackson stares at her for a long moment. "Don't do that."

"What?"

"What are you going to do there?"

Angela blinks back her tears as she replies, "I'm making a documentary on Tibetan art."

"Don't cancel your trip."

"But you said—"

"Take him with you."

"But his schoolwork—"

Jackson removes his glasses and rubs his eyes as he speaks. "Get him away from this place for a while. It would do him a world of good. I'll coordinate it with his teachers and get a reading list so he doesn't fall behind. You two can spend some time together, help him to get his head straight again and he can see a part of the world too few kids even know exists."

Ed, whose head has been swiveling as if he were watching a tennis match, jumps in. "That's a hell of an idea!"

Angela looks at the two men as she wipes her eyes again. "I… I guess I could do that. He's got a passport and… and it's a wonderful idea. Thank you for making it possible."

Jackson almost smiles, "That's why they pay me the big bucks."

Angela looks almost relieved, "About your car…"

"I'll get an estimate tomorrow. Now, let's get Jamie back in here."

GÖNPOY-RI, TIBETAN PLATEAU

It's early morning, and the sun has just broken free of the horizon, bathing the immense mountains with that brilliant light found only in the highest places on the planet.

The intense morning light leaks into a tiny cave. Two simple sleeping mats, a low table, a crude stove and a small, butter lamp-lit shrine are the cave's only furnishings.

In the flickering light of the lamps, two men wrapped in blankets sit in silence, facing the small image of the Buddha below the colorful thangka tapestry. The older, Lama Sang-Nagk, maybe fifty-plus, stirs. The sound of his voice is barely a whisper as he speaks in Tibetan. *"I shall leave today."*

His companion, Lama Wangpo, not yet past his thirties, looks up quizzically. *"Where are you going?"*

"I must prepare for Dampa Garma Pawo."

Lama Wangpo sits up a little straighter. *"I... I didn't know."*

A slight smile tugs at the older lama's lips. *"That this day would ever come?"*

Lama Wangpo is stunned. *"After more than a thousand years… it is finally happening?"*

As Lama Sang-Nagk bows to the shrine and begins to stand, his simple monk's robe opens just a bit revealing a constellation of what one could assume to be tattoos of endless rows of Tibetan mantras across his body, intermixed with various complex images of a type found in this part of the world, all of it having been executed with a remarkably exact precision. The few colors are subdued, yet, even in this fleeting glance, they seem to somehow radiate a faint glow. He snugs his robe, dons a much heavier cloak, then slings a carry bag over his shoulder.

The two men exit their small cave on the mountain's summit and the view is spectacular—they live on the top of the world. The air is filled with the noise of the wind and the snapping of colorful prayer flags.

They clasp hands for a moment, their red robes and jackets fluttering in the wind. Then they lean in and with great respect and affection, touch their foreheads together.

Lama Sang-Nagk turns toward a very unusual kind of a prayer wheel. It is, in fact, the only one of its kind in the entire world. It spins at a smart speed, powered by the rectangular "fins" attached to its circumference that catch the wind. He holds his hands up in respect and bows toward the spinning manifestation of a never-ending series of devout prayers, prayers that have been cast on these winds for over a thousand years.

BABOOM!!!

The deafening sound causes the prayer wheel to momentarily shake, almost as if it were shivering in response to this audible insult.

Both men turn at the sound and the *ROAR* that follows as they watch a jet fighter soar up into the intense blue of the sky.

. . .

The Chinese pilot unsnaps his oxygen mask and roars with laughter. He brings the mask back into position and speaks into its microphone. *"Red Flag base, this is Hawk Two-Two! I can see Devil Mountain! I almost knocked them right off the top!"*

The pilot continues to laugh as he circles the peak. He glances at his altimeter—it reads almost 10,000 meters... *how do the devils breathe up there?*...

He pulls the stick hard over, shoves the throttle forward and turns away from the mountain.

. . .

The two monks seem unaffected by the effects of
the sonic boom, and then the prayer wheel squeaks.
Lama Sang-Nagk quickly moves to an ornately carved
wooden box set near the wheel. He opens a door, and
removes an ancient, long-necked oilcan perched on a
metal stand above several fluttering butter lamps. He
shuts the door and *klick-klock, klick-klock,* precisely oils
the shaft below the whirling fins at its base, then
carefully uses a small rag to clean up the excess.

He turns to Lama Wangpo and shouts above the
noise of the wind, *"That's all it ever needs, but you must
be ever so careful."*

Lama Wangpo, who has been watching all of this
intently, nods that he understands.

Lama Sang-Nagk replaces the oilcan and rag back
inside the wooden box and carefully latches it. He
smiles at his friend, takes a few steps down the well-
worn path, makes his way through a narrow cut
between the rocks... and is gone.

For a long moment, Lama Wangpo looks down
the mountain where his friend has gone. He remembers
the first time he saw him, the stories about how he was
actually over one-hundred years old, how he had been
imprisoned by the invaders, subjected to the most severe

tortures with no effect and had finally just walked out of the prison, the guards unable... or, some had said, unwilling... to stop him. And, of course, how he had taken this poor, wretched orphan monk and helped him to see the true nature of reality, to understand the love and compassion of the Buddhas. Tears begin to well in his eyes... *I will not see you again this lifetime... thank you for your many kindnesses, my true friend...* He wipes his eyes, then turns and walks back to the entrance of the cave.

The prayer wheel suddenly creaks. Lama Wangpo stops and looks back with concern. The wheel becomes quiet of its own accord and continues to silently spin. He stares at the spinning prayer wheel for a long moment. His breathing begins to slow and his eyes half-close. The sound of the wind begins to diminish, the prayer wheel seems to begin to move in slow motion, and the ancient characters inscribed on its face come into focus:

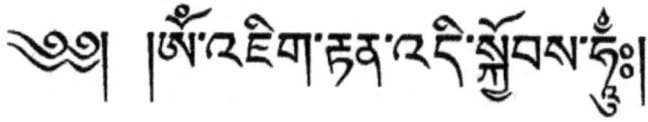

The prayer flags flap in slow motion, revealing that they, too, are inscribed with the same characters, over and over again, the very same characters that had long ago become even an integral part of Lama Sang-Nagk's very body.

Lama Wangpo's eyes open wide. The sound of the wind once again rises. He stands, staring at the spinning prayer wheel for a long moment and then turns and enters the cave.

TIBETAN AUTONOMOUS REGION—SEVERAL
WEEKS LATER

Wind-driven sleet cuts horizontally across the
muddy road as a Land Rover carefully feels its way with
its headlights. On one side is a wall of rock; on the other
a black abyss looms menacingly.

Down the road and around a corner, Lama Sang-
Nagk is walking on the edge of the road, huddled
against the cruel wind, chanting a mantra over and over
above the roar of the violent storm. *"Om Mani Pémé
Hüng, Om Mani Pémé Hüng—"*

He stops walking and chanting and freezes in
place. His face lifts up to the storm and his expression is
one of intensity, as if something had just been revealed.

. . .

Inside the Land Rover, a Chinese driver squints
through the flapping windshield wiper blades as he
puffs at a cigarette hanging from his lips. Sitting next to
him, Chang, an official People's Republic of China guide,
clenches his teeth around his own cigarette in a nervous,
tough-guy posture that doesn't fool anyone. The two
men speak only Chinese to each other. Chang shakes his

head. *"Hiyah! Which Beijing bureaucrat did I piss off to be sent to this despicable place?"*

In the back seat, Angela and Jamie are having their own discussion. "Jamie, you need to do some reading."

"How can I read when we're always bouncing around on some sucky road?"

"Then practice your meditation. It might help your attitude."

Jamie rolls his eyes in response as he flips his legs into a lotus posture and scrunches his face into his version of an exaggeratedly comic meditation pose.

Angela glances up at the two Chinese men through the haze of the smoke while Jamie makes a face and a big deal of fanning the smoke away from his face. "How can I sit when I can't even breathe—?"

The driver suddenly curses out loud and slams on the brakes—there is a THUMP! The image of Lama Sang-Nagk flashes across the windshield as the vehicle begins to spin—his image is replaced by the view of the rock wall, then the black abyss beyond the edge of the road, and the swirling images of the rock wall... black abyss... rock wall... black abyss... and then it stops at the very edge of the drop-off.

The interior of the car is near silent save for the *swish-swish* of the windshield wipers.

Chang is the first to speak and it's a series of splendidly complex Chinese curses.

Jamie looks at his white-faced mother. "Mom! We hit somebody!"

The driver and a furious Chang leap out of the vehicle. Lama Sang-Nagk lies on the side of the road near the edge, terribly injured. Chang and the driver kneel next to him. The driver spits his words, *"What kind of a fool is out in this weather?"*

Chang opens the lama's pitifully ragged over garment, revealing his burgundy robe. *"Just what you'd expect. A monk. The party's always saying religion makes you stupid."* He pulls up the lama's eyelids and looks at the pupils. *"Hmm. He's dead."*

The driver laughs derisively. *"How the hell would you know? You saw that in a movie."*

Angela, with Jamie peering over her shoulder, looks down at the lama. "How badly is he hurt?"

Chang pulls the lama's eyelid back again. "Dead. He's dead."

Jamie is enthralled. "Wow. I never saw a dead guy before."

Angela ignores Jamie. "We should take him to the next village."

The driver looks at Chang. *"What did she say?"*

"She wants to take him to the next village."

"Shit! That's truly stupid. Those people will be really pissed and we'll spend all week filling out reports."

"It's nonsense. Besides, what's the big deal? He's got no wife. He's a monk." He switches to English. "Better to leave him here."

Angela looks at him as if she can't believe what she's hearing. "Leave him here? Why?"

"He's a monk. It's bad luck to move a monk who's died. The local people will know what to do in the morning when they find him."

"In the morning? When they find him?"

Chang flashes a golden-toothed smile. "You don't understand our culture. It's very, very bad luck to move him!"

The two Chinese turn back to the vehicle and begin to examine it for damage as Angela tries to get their attention.

Jamie kneels next to the monk and stares with unabashed curiosity. He tentatively touches the monk's bloody hand. The monk's eyes flutter open.

Lama Sang-Nagk sees Jamie's face appear to sparkle for an instant, and then a circle of glowing Tibetan characters begins to slowly spin in the middle of the boy's forehead. They are the same letters seen earlier on the wheel at the top of the mountain. He stares at the boy... *ah... so it is to be you ...*

He brings his bloody hand with an extended finger to his lips in the universal sign of silence. Jamie's eyes widen—he bites his lip to hold his tongue.

Lama Sang-Nagk painfully tugs at one of several red cords around his neck. Jamie reaches over, gently pulls the cord, and finds a small filigree silver metal box, beautifully detailed with Buddhist symbols. The lama barely nods and Jamie carefully lifts the cord from around the lama's neck. Lama Sang-Nagk points to Jamie and motions for him to put it around his own neck. Jamie stares at the lama for a moment, then slips the cord around his neck and shoves the box down the front of his jacket.

Lama Sang-Nagk smiles, then brings his palms up in the Buddhist greeting. Jamie returns the gesture. He once again brings a finger to his lips, smiles, and then his eyes close. Jamie stares at the lama, not at all sure about what has just happened, wondering... *is he dead now...?*

Angela is still arguing with the two Chinese as they walk back to Jamie.

"Mr. Chang, we can not just leave him here. No one is at fault. It was just an accident so there shouldn't be any problems."

The driver suddenly kneels next to the lama and mutters, "'Scuse." He slips his arms under the lama's body. He stands and takes a step. Suddenly, he fakes a stumble and "trips", and Lama Sang-Nagk's body "slips" from his grasp and falls over the edge of the road into the darkness below.

"Aiyah! I almost fall!"

Chang sees right through the driver's actions and fights back a laugh. "There, you see? We almost lost our driver. Very, very bad luck."

Angela knows exactly what has happened, but she also knows there's nothing to be done. She fights for control and holds her tongue. Chang smiles broadly, nodding his head.

"Okay, we fix our light. We go now." The two Chinese walk back to the vehicle.

Jamie stares over the edge of the road into the darkness below in horror, almost as if he could see something.

Angela looks toward him. "Let's go, Jamie."

Jamie continues to stare into the darkness.

"Jamie, we've got to go."

Jamie continues to stare, "Mom, I... I don't think he was dead. And he just... he just threw him over the edge. I can't believe he did that."

Angela's grim face belies her gentle words as she places an arm around the boy. They walk to the vehicle. "Neither can I, honey."

LHASA, TIBET

In the hills outside the city, Angela and Jamie stand within the roofless ruins of an ancient monastery, videotaping a fading image on a crumbling wall. Jamie is silently transfixed by the breathtakingly beautiful, delicate painting of a four-armed deity; he and the image seem to be contemplating each other.

A shiny new Mercedes sedan pulls up next to their Land Rover. Chang obsequiously opens the back door and greets the occupant; a middle-aged Chinese man wearing a dark blue suit and tie, what remains of his obviously tinted hair carefully slicked back, dark glasses hiding his eyes as he clutches a lit cigarette. Chang can hardly do too much as he assists this apparently important visitor. They walk over to the ruins.

"Missus Angela Edwards, this is Mr. Hsi. He is Chief Administrator of the Tibet Autonomous Region."

Angela looks up from her camera. "Hello, Mr. Hsi."

Mr. Hsi smiles, his English heavily accented. "Hello, nice to meet you. We are very happy to have you show the world our wonderful historical works of art but why are you interested in this old thing? You should film the monasteries we've restored."

"That artwork is new," Angela replies. "I'm interested in what remains in the ancient six-thousand monasteries and nunneries that were destroyed in the Cultural Revolution." She points to the image. "Look at this—whoever the artist was, he had a most marvelous and delicate technique. He created a magnificent Chenrezig, the Buddha of compassion. The Indians call him Avalokiteshvara. Do you know the Chinese name?"

"Of course," Mr. Hsi shrugs. "Kuan-Yin."

Angela is surprised. "You're a Buddhist?"

"My mother. I don't have time for that sort of thing."

"I'm sorry to hear that," Angela observes.

Mr. Hsi's cigarette has burned perilously close to his hand. He takes a deep puff and then tosses the butt aside as he turns to an aide. They speak in whispers for a moment. "I'm afraid that I must go. May I be of other assistance?"

"Yes, thank you," Angela says with a smile. "We'd like to go back to a place on the road a couple of hours from here. It was very beautiful but it was too dark to take any pictures. Would that be possible?"

"Of course. I will arrange it." Mr. Hsi then visibly transforms as he gives Angela his highest wattage smile and makes his move. "Mrs. Edwards, may I be honest?"

Angela looks at him curiously, "Please."

Mr. Hsi continues, "This is simply the most boring place in the world. Nothing like Beijing. However, I'd love to show you our private club. It's at the best hotel on the island. Wonderful food, good music, dancing... I'm quite a good dancer I'm told." His expression is just this side of a leer as he continues to focus his smile.

Angela is momentarily dumbfounded at this obvious and unexpected come-on. She catches herself. "Actually, I... I need to spend some time helping Jamie with his schoolwork. He's fallen quite a bit behind. You know how these children can be! I do appreciate the offer though. Thank you so much."

Mr. Hsi's killer smile now seems a bit strained as he turns to Jamie, regarding him as if he were a pet bug he'd like to squash because he's the only reason he won't be able to parade this sexy western woman in front of his comrades at his club in this desolate, god-forsaken place. "Are you enjoying your visit?"

"Uh huh." Jamie tries to keep his face neutral as he thinks... *you just hit on my Mom you freaking lizard.*

"You should visit Beijing—it's far more interesting."

Mr. Hsi turns, waves goodbye, and enters his car. The vehicle turns and heads back down the road.

Jamie looks at his mother. "Mom! He totally hit on you!"

"Go ahead and rewind it."

"Can I do a download today?"

Angela eyes a group of Chinese soldiers as they walk by. "Let's wait until we get to Dharamsala—they might think we're CIA spies. And after you've made a dent in your reading."

Jamie has finished packing the camera and tripod. As he bends over to pick up the camera, the box Lama Sang-Nagk gave him falls out of his jacket and hangs down by the neck cord.

Angela looks curiously at Jamie. "What's that?"

"Huh?"

Angela walks over and tugs at the pendant. "This."

"Oh. The monk gave it to me right before those guys threw him over the cliff."

"Really? How'd he do that? He was already dead when we got to him, Jamie."

"Chang thought he was dead. While you guys were talking, he opened his eyes, gave me the box, made like he wanted it kept a secret. Then he died; I mean I guess he died. I was afraid to say anything because I didn't want those guys to take it."

Angela closely examines it. "It's a *gau*. Have you opened it?"

"Open it? How do you open it?"

"Don't try. A *gau* usually contains some kind of sacred relic." She glances toward Chang. "Don't let them see it—they'd just take it and try to sell it. It's probably very important to his people."

Jamie nods, "Then we need to get it back to them."

"Well, since the Chinese won't let us talk to the real monks," she winks, "… maybe in Dharamsala." She brings a finger to her lips, just like Lama Sang-Nagk did. "After we find his body."

. . .

The Land Rover pulls over to the side of the road near the spot where Lama Sang-Nagk was hit several nights ago. Angela, Jamie and the two Chinese step out. There's a river at the bottom of the cliff with a rocky beach.

The driver turns and spits. *"What in the hell are we doing back here?"*

Chang shrugs, *"She wants to take pictures."*

They watch as Angela and Jamie unload her camera equipment and another bag. When Angela opens it, she pulls out two long climbing ropes.

The driver throws his hands up in despair, *"Shit! This is going to be trouble!"*

Chang calmly turns to his friend and hands him his cell phone, *"You can express your concerns directly to Mr. Hsi himself, if you like."* He turns to Angela. "What are you doing, Missus Angela?"

Angela has looped the rope through the side windows of the Land Rover and over the vehicle's top. She tosses the remaining coils of the rope over the edge of the road.

"Can't see anything from up here."

Jamie nervously watches her rig a second rope. "What's that for?"

"You want to come, don't you?"

. . .

A few minutes later, Angela, wearing a backpack, and Jamie are rappelling down the step slope. Angela is below Jamie and is controlling her descent with one hand as she keeps another on Jamie's rope, just in case.

"You're doing great, Jamie!"

"Yeah, right!"

"Just imagine what your moron friends at school would think if they could see you now!"

"They'd know we're both crazy!"

. . .

At the bottom of the cliff, Angela and Jamie step out of their ropes. Jamie looks up—the two Chinese men seem a very long way up the steep slope. "Mom, how are we going to get back up?"

"It's a little slower than coming down."

"Where did you learn to do this kind of stuff?"

Angela pauses as she sorts out the equipment. "Your father." She looks up, slings the camera over her shoulder and then begins to walk toward a field of boulders. Jamie falls in behind her.

As they make their way past a large boulder, Jamie looks around. "I bet somebody already found him—."

They both freeze as they see the lama's bloody clothing draped on a rock, as if the wearer had dissolved from within them. Angela looks around and kind of squints, not sure she's actually seeing what her eyes seem tell her—that the entire area surrounding the clothing, including Jamie and herself, is within the midst of a hemisphere of light, the border of which defines the faintest of the colors of the rainbow.

Jamie's voice is a whisper, "This is weird."

Angela is also caught up in the moment and answers in a whisper. "When I wave at you, walk over and kneel down next to his clothes. Keep them in the shot."

She begins to shoot, then waves at Jamie. Jamie slowly walks over and kneels next to the lama's clothing. He looks down. A shirtsleeve protrudes just a bit from the ends of a coat sleeve. At the end of the shirt sleeve, lying neatly on the ground, are four fingernails and a thumbnail. The other sleeve is folded across the chest and the nails lie exactly where a hand should be.

"Umm."

Jamie almost jumps out of his skin at the sound of the old man's voice. He looks around. To his left, near an overhanding boulder, Lama Sang-Nagk sits in the shadows. He's now dressed in white robes, the beads of his *mala* moving over his right hand as his thumb rhythmically pulls them down, one at a time.

Jamie silently stares at the old man as Angela joins him, still shooting video.

The old man smiles. "It's good to see you again."

Jamie is stunned. "You're still alive? You speak English?"

Lama Sang-Nagk laughs as if this is the funniest thing he has ever heard.

Angela keeps shooting as she speaks. "How long have you been here?"

"Since we last met, of course." He pauses, "When you take my things—."

Jamie is wide-eyed. "You... you fell all the way... you're—."

Lama Sang-Nagk continues, "... you must carefully pick up all of my hair, fingernails and toenails. That's all that's really left. Keep them together with my clothing. The lamas will want to examine them. And don't forget the *gau*."

Jamie's hand involuntarily goes to the metal box.

Angela asks, "Which lamas?"

"The next lamas you speak with."

"In Dharamsala?"

"Umm." There's kind of a shimmer around Lama Sang-Nagk, and *he suddenly transforms into a fierce-looking, longhaired woman warrior* for just a moment... and then he's gone.

Jamie blinks, looks around, "Where is he?" He runs around the side of the boulder. He reappears from the other side as Angela hunkers down and looks under the overhang. She turns to Jamie, who looks very spooked. "Mom! That was the guy we hit! It's him!"

Angela is clearly disturbed. She turns back to the clothing. "I've got plastic bags in my pack. Please get them for me." Jamie is frozen in place, looking where Lama Sang-Nagk last appeared. "Jamie, get the bags."

Jamie snaps out of it and goes for the bags. Angela quickly rewinds the video and begins to review it. As the screen lights up, there is... nothing. No rainbow colors, no images of the lama. Just Jamie, seeming to be looking at and talking to... nothing.

Jamie runs up with the bag. "Mom, it was him!"

She nods as she continues to stare at the screen. "Yes, it was."

GÖNPOY-RI, TIBETAN PLATEAU

It is night and the prayer wheel is shrieking almost as loudly as the wind. Sheets of snow blast Lama Wangpo as he struggles in the darkness to position a stick near the bottom of the prayer wheel's shaft, while at the same time avoiding the madly whirling fins.

"Almost... just a little push..."

A terrific flash of lightning is immediately followed by a blast of thunder. Lama Wangpo's grip is shaky and the stick slips. A fin smacks the stick, flinging it into the monk's head. He falls to his knees, blood streaming from an open gash.

The prayer wheel begins to physically shudder, even as the shrieking increases in volume. Lama Wangpo looks up through his blood-covered eyes as the wind whips his robes around his body, watching with terrified fascination as the inconceivable begins to happen.

He drops back on his buttocks into a posture of meditation, in the middle of the fury of the storm, hands on his knees, and begins to chant in a surprisingly strong and deeply resonant voice, a voice that seems octaves lower than we've heard before yet resonant with overtones, that joins in with an identical chant coming from... somewhere?

"Om Ah Hüng—"

Another flash of lightning, a blast of thunder, and the wildly vibrating prayer wheel self-destructs in a paroxysm of violence that sends a piece of the shaft slashing directly into the young lama's chest. He is knocked backwards and lies face-up, staring into the savage sky with open eyes. As they finally close, the howling wind rips one end of the madly flapping cord of prayer flags loose. The cord and its flags lash about in the wind, and then the other end breaks free.

For a moment, the freed cord and flags catch on the dead lama's body, but then they quickly blow away into the tempestuous night.

. . .

Many millions of miles from the earth, a solid mass of rock some sixteen kilometers in diameter experiences a perturbation in its orbit. It gently brushes against a more massive neighbor twice its size, thirty-two kilometers in diameter. The contact is barely a collision, a gentle brush that raises just a bit of dust that almost instantly settles, just enough to alter the larger body's orbit in such a way as to cause it to begin to depart its old neighborhood.

DHARAMSALA, INDIA

Samten Rinpoche sits on a cushion at a low table, intently peering through his glasses at the papers in front of him. He's a round man, rather like a fireplug, not so short but quite thick, graceful fingers holding a pen with one hand as he delicately works a wooden back-scratcher with the other, shrugging within his saffron-colored robes to reach that special spot needing attention. Like many Tibetans, his boyish face belies his more than half-century of this current existence. He looks up as he hears the *swish* of the curtain across the entrance to the room.

Angela enters, hands clasped in greeting. Rinpoche smiles broadly, returning her greeting, his voice slightly colored with a bit of a singsong British flavor. "Angela! Come in! How good to see you!" Angela sits on the cushions in front of the low table. Samten Rinpoche sighs as he puts down his pen. "I am awash in paperwork. So many refugees to care for! How have you been?"

"My son and my work keep me very busy. By the way, he came with me this time."

"Wonderful! Where is he?"

"He'll be here shortly. Rinpoche, I'm worried sick about him."

"How so?"

"He's getting into trouble. It's my fault… I don't spend enough time with him. That, plus he still misses his father so much… and so do I."

Rinpoche smiles, then starts to chuckle. "Just today I was thinking of the time Jake got us the building supplies." Angela smiles at the memory. The Rinpoche tilts his head as he tries to remember, "He played… what do you call it?"

"Poker."

"Yes, poker. He won so much money." He starts to giggle, motioning for her to continue the story. She starts to laugh herself as she continues. "He… he told the man he'd do him a favor and let him take it as a tax deduction. And he did." They both collapse into laughter, wiping their eyes.

"Your husband was such a good friend to us. And so are you."

"I think Jamie resents that Jake died over here. He really didn't want to come with me."

"He's still so young. His father is gone. He misses him. How could he understand? Would you like for me to speak with him?"

"Jake had taught him meditation. He was doing so well with it but after Jake died, he just gave it up. Anything you can—"

She stops as Rinpoche waves toward the door. "Ah, you must be Jamie. Please, come in!" Jamie walks in and sits next to his mother. She turns to Jamie, "This is Samten Rinpoche."

The lama holds out his hand for a western handshake. Jamie places the notebook he's been carrying on Rinpoche's table and shakes his hand. "I am so happy to meet you. Are you enjoying your stay?"

"Yeah. It's interesting."

"What do you like best?"

"The paintings. I've only seen photos before. They're awesome." Jamie points to a thangka depicting a thousand-armed figure. "That one's really amazing."

Rinpoche squints at the thangka hanging next to a picture of the Dalai Lama, then he turns to Angela with a knowing look. "That particular thangka was your father's favorite. It is Avalokiteshvara, the Buddha of compassion. We often call him Chenrezig. There's a wonderful story about him. Do you know it?"

"No."

"Avalokiteshvara is one of the greatest bodhisattvas—one whose every thought and act is to help other beings attain enlightenment."

"You said 'is'. He's still around?"

Rinpoche gently laughs. "Of course. He's a Buddha; they are always everywhere. Now, knowing that helping all beings attain enlightenment would be a big job, he said that if he ever became discouraged, then, '… may I be shattered into a thousand pieces.'" Guess what happened?"

Jamie responds, "He broke into a thousand pieces" as if it was obvious.

"Exactly!"

"He just kind of exploded?"

"Yes, but the great Amitabha Buddha blessed him and told him that he must never give up on the beings of this world. And then he helped him to become even more than whole again." Jamie looks back over at the image as Rinpoche continues to speak. "That's why he has a thousand arms, a thousand eyes and nine heads, so that he can see everywhere and not miss a thing, and do even more to help all beings."

"My father helped somebody and it got him killed."

Rinpoche studies the boy for a moment. "Your father, Jamie, understood compassion as few men do."

"Sounds to me like if you try to help people you either blow up or die."

Rinpoche's voice softens. "Not always, Jamie. Most people die while doing nothing in particular."

"Yeah, shit happens."

Angela looks up in horror. "Jamie!"

Rinpoche gently holds up his hand. "You are correct. Shit happens. Life is very unpredictable. There are many things we neither know nor fully understand. What counts in the end is how we have lived it. And how we are."

Jamie stares at the lama for a long quiet moment. Angela breaks the silence. "Show him what the monk gave you."

Jamie reaches into his shirt and pulls the *gau* from around his neck.

Rinpoche's demeanor becomes more serious as Jamie tries to hand it to him. "Please, put it on the table." Jamie does as he's asked. "Where did you get this?"

"Our Chinese driver hit a monk on the road. He was dying, and he asked me to take it. He didn't want the other two guys to know he'd given it to me."

Rinpoche pauses for a moment. "I see. Excuse me." He calls out, "Chö-Nyi!" A young monk instantly enters. Rinpoche speaks to him in Tibetan, *"Quickly, summon Chökli Rinpoche! Ask him to please hurry!"*

The young monk turns and silently exits the room. "I have sent for Chökli Rinpoche. It will be just a moment."

Almost before he stops speaking, Chökli Rinpoche enters and bows in greeting. He is a picture of contradictions: obviously quite old yet radiating physical strength and vitality, his tied-up long grey hair and pointed scraggly beard give him a kind of wild ferocity. At the same time, there's a playful twinkle in his eyes as he glances around the room. Samten Rinpoche rises and pulls another cushion out for his old friend. He turns to Angela and Jamie. "This is Chökli Rinpoche." He turns to the two westerners, "This is Angela and Jamie Edwards."

The old lama's fierce face cracks with a huge smile as he holds his hands up in greeting, then sits next to Samten Rinpoche. Samten Rinpoche holds his upturned palm toward the *gau*. *"It was given to the boy."*

Chökli Rinpoche sits in silence for a long moment, staring at the *gau*. Then his eyes fall on to Jamie's notebook. The cover is filled with strange doodles that resemble the graffiti Jamie sprayed on Mr. Jackson's car. He looks at Jamie. "Did you write these things?"

Jamie nods. "Yeah. I was just playing around. They don't mean anything."

Chökli Rinpoche silently stares at the boy for a long moment, then instructs, "Please pick up the *gau* and hold it in your palm." Chökli Rinpoche pantomimes his instructions as he speaks. Jamie does as he's shown.

"Now, take your other hand and press the middle of each short side with your fingertips."

Jamie presses the sides, and the top of the *gau* suddenly flips open. His eyes widen with excitement. "That's pretty cool!"

Chökli Rinpoche looks into the *gau* and sighs as he nods. Inside nestles a piece of bone, carved with the same characters seen earlier on the mountaintop prayer wheel and flags:

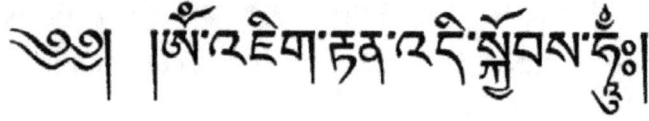

Angela turns to Chökli Rinpoche. "May I?"

He motions for Angela to look, saying, "Please insure that your breath does not touch it."

She glances in, shielding her mouth, as does Samten Rinpoche. Angela looks up at Chökli Rinpoche, "What does the inscription say?"

"It's something about 'saving the world'." Chökli Rinpoche then motions for Jamie to place the open *gau* next to the "doodles" on his notebook. There is a striking similarity, as if Jamie had been attempting to crudely copy the carefully carved characters.

Angela looks at Jamie. "Have you seen these characters before?"

"I don't know. I don't think so."

Angela looks at the two Rinpoches. "He must have, don't you think?"

The Rinpoches turn to each other. Chökli Rinpoche nods, *"Lama Sang-Nagk has passed."*

Samten Rinpoche sighs. *"Yes. What does this mean?"*

"Something has happened to the Korlo Gön-Poy. If it has stopped, we have precious little time to do many things."

He turns to Jamie. "Please close the *gau*." Jamie carefully closes the box. "Keep the *gau* and its contents secret. You must not show it to anyone else. And of course, no one, not even you, must touch it, even with your breath, until the proper time."

Jamie's eyes brighten, "I get to keep it?"

"For now," Chökli Rinpoche responds, "… its safekeeping is your responsibility."

"What is it?" Jamie asks.

"It is a prayer, and a very important and sacred relic." He turns to Angela, "Where is the body of Lama Sang-Nagk?"

"Our Chinese driver accidentally slipped and 'lost' it over the edge of a cliff next to the road that night during a storm. Jamie and I went back for it the next day." She takes a large package out of her backpack and removes the contents. She places the clothing on the desk and then two small plastic bags—one containing bits of hair and one with the fingernails and toenails.

"This is all that remained. All of it, the clothing, the nails and the hair were lying as if his body had simply dissolved. And there was a... I don't know how to describe it... a kind of rainbow light around the place where we found these."

Jamie and Angela glance at each other, each wondering how to describe the rest. Jamie breaks the silence. "Go ahead, Mom. Tell him."

Angela continues. "The clothing he wore on the night of the accident was empty on the ground, but there he was, dressed in glowing white robes, sitting in the rocks to one side. I don't know any other way to say this—it was him, and he spoke to us."

Both lamas are silent for a moment. Samten Rinpoche is the first to speak as he looks at Jamie, "And you also saw this?"

"Yeah! I couldn't believe it! Plus he spoke perfect English. I had this weird feeling like I met him before or something. He said to bring all of this stuff to the lamas. And then he turned into this awesome warrior woman... and he disappeared. I've never seen anything like it ever."

Angela points to her camera. "I took a video of what we saw. The rainbow doesn't show up and neither does he. Not a trace. I can't explain it."

Both lamas are silent for another long moment. Samten Rinpoche is the first to speak, "Lama Sang-Nagk was a yogi of great accomplishment and a being of tremendous importance. Sometimes when these very special ones leave their bodies for good, they transform into beings of pure light. All that remains are the impurities, the nails and hair. It is a very, very rare thing to observe. You have been most fortunate." He pauses for a moment as he reverently touches the clothing. There are tears in his eyes as he turns to Angela. "The fact that you are the ones he chose, and that you have brought his remains to us are very auspicious events." He silently stares at the mother and her son, thinking... *you can't even begin to know how this changes... everything...*

"So, I think we are finished for now?"

Angela and Jamie stand, followed by the two Rinpoches, who bring their hands up to their hearts. Angela and Jamie return the gesture.

As they start to leave the room, Jamie glances over to a small shrine. Standing on the shrine below another image of the Buddha is a black and white photo of a western man.

"Is that my Dad?"

Lama Samten smiles, "Yes, it is your father." Jamie crosses to the shrine to get a better look. "You may pick it up if you like."

Jamie carefully picks up the framed photograph. "I've never seen this one. What's it here for?"

"He was our good friend. We pray for his well-being and fortunate rebirth."

"Rebirth? Like reincarnation?"

Samten Rinpoche smiles as he nods.

"You mean my Dad could come back? I could actually see him again?"

"It is a very complex thing, Jamie. And even if you did meet, you might not even recognize him... or her."

Jamie replaces the photo and stares at it for a long moment. Then, obviously a little confused, he turns and walks to his waiting mother. He turns back to Rinpoche, "But it's possible?"

Rinpoche smiles and gently shrugs.

Jamie nods, "Nice to meet you," and then he and Angela turn and leave the room.

The two Rinpoches silently stand, and then a look of somber, great resignation passes between them. Samten Rinpoche is the first to speak, *"Surely he wasn't alone up there."*

"No. Lama Wangpo was with him. I don't believe you knew him."

"Knew?"

"I don't think he's with us any longer, either."

. . .

It's late afternoon, and the fiery display of the afternoon sun dramatically colors the sky. Jamie sits on the flat rooftop, working with his notebook computer. A small Tibetan toddler sits next to him, apparently fascinated by this pale-skinned westerner.

Angela and a teenaged Tibetan monk appear from the stairwell below. She smiles at her son as she speaks, "How's it going?"

"Almost done."

Angela nods toward the child, "Who's your friend?"

"I don't know. I was working and when I looked up, he was sitting there. He keeps staring at me."

The young monk reaches down and touches the boy, "His name is Jikme. He's my half brother. He thinks it's funny to hide from me."

The boy looks up at Angela and his face breaks into a huge smile. Angela can't help herself; she bends down and picks the youngster up. He wraps his little arms around her neck. "Oh my goodness, you're just a little lover aren't you?... Sorry, Tseten, this is my son, Jamie."

Tseten smiles as he nods to Jamie. "Hello."

Jamie sticks out his hand and the boys shake. "Hi."

Angela shifts the child to one arm. "One of Tseten's duties is to take care of the monastery's computers. And he's interested in astronomy."

Tseten glances at Jamie's computer screen. "Ho! I use this software! It's very good, isn't it?"

Jamie's demeanor instantly changes—he's really into this. "Nothing else comes close. Right now I'm downloading my data file from the observatory. They have this program where you can request telescope time. They'll schedule it to look where you want for whatever time you can get, and then send you the images."

"Anyone can do this?"

"Umm, not really—"

Angela jumps in, "Jamie won the telescope time as a science award." She starts to hand Jikme to Tseten but the child's eyes are locked on hers as his hands touch her face here and there, as if searching for something. "Well, you're just a sweetheart, aren't you? I have to go now, okay?"

Tseten reaches up and takes the child from Angela.

She turns back to Jamie. "I'll come get you when it's dinner time."

"Okay."

Angela disappears back down the stairs. The computer beeps. Jamie nods in approval, "Cool. I can log off."

"What will you do now?"

"Analyze the data. See what I got. I'd almost bet anything I found an unknown double-star cluster earlier this year, but I wanted to check it with a bigger telescope. Come on by later and I'll show you what it looks like. The images should be really cool." Jamie closes the lid on the computer. "You live in the monastery?"

"Yes."

Jamie does a double take, "You're a monk?"

"Yes."

"Where's your family?"

"My mother lives in Leh. My father was killed by the Chinese."

"Wow, you must really hate them."

"I did. Then I heard His Holiness, the Dalai Lama say that you must practice compassion toward those who you see as your enemies as much as for those whom you love the most. I pray for the Chinese, that they may be freed from their ignorance."

"Dude, I would be so pissed. I'd want to kill every one of them. How do you do it?"

Tseten give a little laugh. "It takes a lot of practice."

"What about this Aval... Avalo... the one with a thousand arms and eyes and all that?

"Avalokiteshvara. The Buddha of compassion."

"You really believe in all that stuff?"

Tseten smiles. "Like showing compassion to all beings and helping when we can? Yes."

Jamie picks up his computer and starts to walk toward the stairwell. "Still... your Dad..." He pauses for a moment, then picks it up again, "You believe in reincarnation?"

"Those I greatly respect say that it is. I don't know that it isn't."

Jamie pauses as he considers Tseten's answer. "You guys have an interesting way of explaining stuff. So you think you'll see your father again?"

"As my father was? I don't think that's the way it works."

Jamie looks at Tseten for a moment... *I like this guy but he's really different...* "I better get going." He heads for the stairs. "Don't forget to come by tonight and I'll show you the images."

"Thank you. I will."

Jamie heads down the stairs as Tseten, still holding the child, watches him disappear.

. . .

Inside the tiny but cozy room, Angela reads by the light of a small lamp as Jamie works on his laptop as he sits on his sleeping pad. Neither speaks, both lost in their concentration.

There's a knock at the door. Jamie looks up. "I'll get it." He crosses over and opens the door—it's Tseten. "Hi. Come on in."

Tseten enters, "Hi", and half-bows toward Angela, "Hello, Missus Angela."

Angela smiles back. "Hi, Tseten. Jikme didn't escape again, did he?"

"Oh no! I came to see Jamie's images." He turns to Jamie. "Your pictures were good?"

Jamie pulls the computer toward them. "Take a look." Tseten squats down and stares at the screen. "Here's what we got." He points to four frames of star field imagery shown on the screen. The cursor moves to a central spot on the first. "This is what I wanted to see and it's definitely not a double star." The cursor moves to a corner of the first frame, right under a tiny "smudge." "But look at this."

"What is it?"

"I thought it was just a bad pixel. But look at the other three images. Each one was taken an hour after the previous shot." The four separate shots move by in sequence. The smudge is a little further toward the center of each successive frame.

Tseten looks again. "Oh. It is something. And it is moving."

Jamie nods. "And that means it's either moving really fast and far away—"

"Or not so fast and close."

"Hey, you're pretty good at this!" Jamie holds out his fist. Tseten just looks at it. "You're supposed to do this." He shows him the fist bang/tap/grab routine. Tseten laughs and they try it again.

Angela has come up behind the two boys. "Did you look it up?"

"It's not in the catalogue."

"Can you get another look?"

"I've still got ten hours left in my account. Can I use the satphone?"

"Sure."

"Great. Come on, Tseten; let's see if we can figure out where it'll be tomorrow night. And I need to send a message to Dr. Johansson. He's my mentor."

"Mentor? Like a teacher?"

"Yeah. Like a teacher."

KITT PEAK OBSERVATORY, ARIZONA

The last colors of a desert sunset give way to the blue-black of the coming night. Dr. Edward Johansson, Ph.D.'s brisk gait and lanky frame belie his years—this is a man who loves going to work. He strides toward the observatory entrance and enters.

. . .

Ginny Kagel, Dr. Johansson's graduate student assistant, looks up from her computer as he enters. "Hi, Doc."

"Hi, Ginny. Anything worth looking at?" They both laugh at the joke—*everything* in the sky is worth looking at to an astronomer.

"We got an e-mail from your young protégé."

"Which one?"

"Jamie Edwards."

"Ah, Jamie. Did he find his double star?"

"No, but he thinks he's maybe found something else. He attached the images from his last session and wants to take another look. Want to see them?"

"Why don't you take a look first? We don't want him to waste his remaining viewing time. I'll be in the imaging room." Dr. Johansson exits through a different door.

. . .

Dr. Johansson sits in the darkened, red-lit room at a bank of video monitors and telescope controls. He watches the images of the night sky on the various monitors as he taps on a keyboard and moves a joystick.

Ginny enters the room. "You need to see this."

Dr. Johansson fine-tunes a setting as he speaks, "What'cha got?"

"I've put Jamie's images on number two." Ginny taps on another keyboard, and Jamie's images now appear. Jamie's object of interest is highlighted inside a marking square.

Dr. Johansson reaches over to Ginny's keyboard and begins to type. A window opens to one side of the screen and numbers fly by as he enters his data. He keeps typing as he speaks, "Did you look it up?"

"Yep. It's not listed."

"Oh my... go ahead and set up a viewing schedule. In fact, let's use my block for tonight. Better contact Cambridge and log it in right now before someone else sees it. We don't want Jamie to lose his chance for immortality."

DHARAMSALA

The main shrine room in the monastery is quite
large with an ornately elaborate shrine centered at one
end. All of the walls are covered with brocade thangkas,
and incense floats in he air. A low droning chant from a
group of saffron-robed monks fills the room as Chökli
Rinpoche enters.

To his front, Samten Rinpoche sits to one side of
the monks, his body slowly swaying in time with the
rhythm of the chanting, and then he turns his head and
looks at Chökli Rinpoche as if he'd been called by name.
The two Rinpoche's eyes meet. Samten Rinpoche
stands, bows to the statue of the Buddha, and walks to
the back of the room. They sit next to each other.
Samten Rinpoche whispers, *"I know so little of this
tradition. What are the words again?"*

*"'A fiery death to all but the lowliest of beings'.
There are many possibilities."*

"Such as?"

"Frankly, I always thought of a nuclear war."

Samten Rinpoche silently considers what he's
heard, then tilts his head in curiosity, *"Ah, that again.
You know, Rinpoche, I've often wondered, if one were to
be caught up in a nuclear explosion, do you think the*

consciousness would survive? If all of the very smallest of particles of one's being were instantly destroyed, it's hard to imagine how there could be enough... enough of anything to allow for the transference to take place."

Chökli Rinpoche shakes his head, *"I've wondered that myself. I'm inclined to think that what we consider to be an instant may not be an instant at that moment, and that whatever it is that actually constitutes pure consciousness, does not rely on any mode of physicality, or any kind physical attributes for that matter. Of course, that's just me wondering about the unknowable."* The two men sit for a moment, and then Chökli Rinpoche continues, *"But now, I am also reminded of something Drolma Pa-Mo once said."*

"Drolma! You have seen her since her escape?"

"Once, while she was recovering at Tsering Ling, just before she asked to go into retreat in Ladakh. She once said that when she performed the visualization, 'it', whatever 'it' is, comes from another place. Perhaps from another world."

"Something not of this earth?"

"Yes."

Samten Rinpoche silently considers his friend's words. *"The father, now the son. He is certainly a part of this."*

"And Drolma, of course."

Samten Rinpoche looks at his friend for a long moment. *"Of course."*

SANTA MONICA BEACH, LOS ANGELES

Ed and a group of mostly very fit women are just finishing their training run along the beach. Tycho, a beautiful golden retriever, runs next to Ed, unleashed, wearing a colorful bandanna around his neck.

The group slows to a walk to cool down, and they stop to get some water. Ed pours some of the water over his head. "Good run, ladies!"

A redhead kneels next to Tycho, takes a drink from her water bottle and then turns to the dog. "Here sweetie, your turn." She starts to squirt water into the panting dog's mouth and he laps it up, loving it.

A blonde scratches Tycho's ears. "You're a good runner, Tycho. Yes you are!"

Ed looks on jealously. "Hey, what about me?"

The blonde laughs. "Scratch your own ears, Ed!"

Ed's cell phone begins to ring. He pulls it off of his water belt and answers. "Hello." There's a pause, then "Hey! Where are you?"

. . .

Angela sits on the monastery's rooftop, watching the rising dawn. She glances at a photo of Jamie, herself, and her late husband. "It's a beautiful dawn. I wish you were her with us."

Ed's voice can be heard from the telephone, "Thinking about Jake, aren't you?"

"I see him everywhere here. God, I miss him."

"Me too, honey. How's Jamie?"

"It's like night and day. Bringing him was a great idea. And he's got something to tell you. Hold on and say hi to him."

. . .

Angela enters their room and sees that Jamie has just opened his eyes. "Come up and say hi to your granddad." He crawls out of bed, finds his shoes and follows her back up to the roof.

Jamie takes the phone from Angela, and switches to the speaker. "Hi, Grandpa! Whatcha' doing? Is Tycho okay?"

"That's a nice change. You asked about me before that old fleabag. Tycho's right here. Want to say hi?"

"I'd rather tell you. I discovered anew asteroid! It's called 2014 BD."

"Yeah? You trip over it while you were out hiking?"

"C'm on Grandpa, it's in outer space! Millions of miles away!"

"Get outta' here! Hey, wait a minute. Why didn't they call it 'Jamie BD' or something like that?"

"Maybe they will later."

"How the hell did you get so smart, kid? Wow, that's just super. Hey, what's it like over there?"

"Really different. Nice people and they've got awesome art. Some of the paintings are so amazing—they'd make really cool tattoos."

"Great. When you get back, we'll both go out and get tattoos. Really freak your mother out."

Angela rolls her eyes as she hears this and shakes her head in faux despair.

Ed continues, "How's the food?"

"Basically, it sucks but you get used to it. You out running with your girlfriends?"

. . .

The door to Angela's room opens. Tseten carefully guides Jikme into the room, then gently closes the door, leaving the child alone.

. . .

The women on the beach pet Tycho and talk among themselves as Ed continues his call. "It's great. Quiet for a change with you two out of the house."

Jamie's voice can be heard. "Yeah, sure. You miss us. Don't worry, we'll be back in a couple of weeks."

Ed laughs. "Thanks for the warning. Okay, pal, have a blast and listen, I really am proud of you. Take care of yourself and your Mom."

"I will. I miss you."

"Me too. Bye." Ed hangs up the phone.

The blonde walks over. "Was that Jamie?"

"Yep. God, that kid's just amazing. Discovered himself an asteroid."

The blonde is impressed, "Wow."

Ed smiles as he shakes his head. "That's one way of putting it."

. . .

Angela walks into her room to find Jikme on the floor with her jewelry roll. "Where did you—?" Angela stops as she watches the child. He intently searches through the earrings, bracelets, pendants and then stops.

His chubby fingers reach in and fumble a bit to pick out a pair of jade earrings. He clasps them and looks up at Angela, beaming.

"You like those too? They're my favorites. My husband gave them to me." She is interrupted by a knock on the door—it's a mildly annoyed Tseten.

"I am very sorry. He escaped from me again."

"It's all right. We were just getting acquainted."

Tseten gently starts to take the earrings from the child, but Jikme pulls them away, then hands them to Angela himself.

"This is not like him. He never touches anyone's things."

"Please, he can play with anything he likes."

Tseten looks at the earrings with interest.

"They are very beautiful."

"Thank you. My husband got them for me on one of his visits here."

"Ah, I see… well, he needs to have his breakfast now. Sorry for any inconvenience."

Angela hugs the child and smiles. "This little sweetheart could never be an inconvenience."

Tseten picks up the child and steps through the door. Angela watches as the door closes, then looks at the earrings for a long moment.

. . .

Angela sits with Samten Rinpoche and Chökli Rinpoche in the office as they watch two Tibetan men open a laptop and position it for viewing. One of the men taps on the keyboard and a slightly grainy video begins to play.

A monk walks out of a building followed by a companion and sits on the sidewalk. The companion reaches into his overcoat and brings out a large plastic jug. He opens the jug, and pours the contents over the monk, who looks up, smiles and nods. The man then hands the monk a lighter. The monk lights the lighter and drops it next to himself. He erupts in flames—yet he doesn't react. The other man then unfurls a banner, written in English, Chinese and Tibetan, that reads "Free Tibet And Its People Now!".

In a matter of seconds, they are surrounded by police who try to beat out the flames, and then throw the second man to the ground as they arrest him...

The Rinpoches and the two men immediately begin to chant, *"Om Mani Pémé Hüng, Om Mani Pémé Hüng..."*

Angela holds her clenched fists to her mouth in horror as she watches the video, unable to tear her eyes away. She tries to speak, but can only say, "Oh my God... oh my God..."

Jamie suddenly enters, computer under one arm, a worried look on his face. Angela looks up as Chökli Rinpoche quickly closes the screen on the laptop. "Yes, Jamie, what's wrong?"

"I need talk to you."

Angela turns to the others. "Please excuse us." She stands and takes Jamie out onto the front steps. They sit, and she asks, "What is it?"

"I downloaded my observations. We've got a lot more data now." Jamie flips open his computer. Angela leans in and watches as her son brings the images to life. An almost spherically shaped object fills the screen.

"This is 2014 BD. It's about thirty-two kilometers in diameter. It's got to have a mass of several billion tons. It's freaking huge!"

The image shifts to a page of orbital calculations.

"Here's the orbital data based on what we've got so far."

Angela shakes her head, "Those numbers make my eyes cross. What do they mean?"

Jamie taps the keyboard. The image now shows a portion of the solar system with a dotted line passing across it. "I wanted to see how close it would come to us." There's more tapping on the keys and then the earth's orbit appears on the image. The two lines cross. The angle of view shifts ninety degrees to another perspective. The lines still cross. "See where the two lines cross? They cross at the same place... at the same time... on the same date."

Angela's face reflects the intensity with which she hears her son's words.

"It's gonna hit us, Mom.   On December 31st. Happy New Year."

"Are you sure?"

"Mom, it's celestial mechanics. You just plug in the numbers. It's math."

"Are you really sure?   Are the numbers all correct?"

"The margin of error is less than fifteen miles and it's only going to get smaller. Mom, that thing is so freaking big. If it hits us..."

Angela wraps an arm around Jamie. "Come on, let's go call Dr. Johansson."

Chapter 2

REACTION

KITT PEAK OBSERVATORY, ARIZONA, MARCH 1

The normally quiet, desert night is under a media siege. Satellite news trucks are parked outside of the observatory, bright lights glare and reporters jostle for position.

The doors to the main building open and Dr. Johansson walks outside with an ashen-faced Ginny. He flinches at the bright lights and holds up a hand to protect his eyes. "Please, your lights are ruining our observations."

A reporter shoves a mike in his face. "Dr. Johansson, is it true that 2014 BD will collide with the earth on December 31st?" The clamoring of the reporters suddenly dies down as they all wait for an answer.

"From what we now know, there is a high probability of a—"

"Doctor, can you please just give us a yes or no?"

"The present data gives us a ninety-nine-point-nine percent chance of a collision." Suddenly, it is very quiet.

A second reporter holds his mike out. "What would be the effect of such a collision?"

"This could be a solid piece of rock some 32 kilometers, that's about 20 miles, in diameter. If that's the case, it has a mass of roughly three billion metric tons. When it arrives, it will be traveling at a relative speed of about 61,000 miles per hour. Any contact with the earth would be catastrophic. The more direct the collision, the more catastrophic the results."

Yet another reporter chimes in. "Won't it burn up in the atmosphere?"

Dr. Johansson pauses for a moment, "It might lose a few tens of feet of its diameter."

One reporter seems to hear what Dr. Johansson is really saying. "If it's a direct hit, does this mean the end of life on earth?" You could hear a pin drop.

"I… I don't really know."

"What about the human race?"

"We are a fragile species. We've been _very_ lucky so far.

"Has our luck run out?"

"I can't answer that."

"Who is Jamie Edwards?"

"He's... he's out of the country. I'm sorry, but I must go. Please turn your lights out so that we can use our telescopes. As you can imagine, we are very busy at this time." Dr. Johansson and Ginny turn and go back inside, leaving the news crews, their trucks and generators. Then, one by one, the media lights begin to flick off until the night is dark once again.

THE WHITE HOUSE, WASHINGTON, D.C.

President Samuels, in shirtsleeves with a loosened tie, sits on a couch in the Oval Office as he watches the interview with Dr. Johansson conclude. "Does the good doctor know what he's talking about?"

Rich Bradshaw, the President's national security advisor looks up from a handful of notes. "Space Command says he's the expert."

The President rubs his eyes as he speaks, "Damn, where'd this thing come from?"

Bradshaw glances at his notes. "Best guess is out of the asteroid belt between Mars and Jupiter."

"I thought we had a program to look for these things."

"We do. You cut the funding though."

"Why the hell did I do that?"

"To fund a methanol plant for Senator Robbins. Remember? The Thompson bill? We needed his vote?"

"Let's keep that to ourselves," the President sighs. "Who found it?"

"Jamie Edwards. He's a ninth or tenth-grade science whiz in Los Angeles. His mother makes documentary films. They've been traveling in India and Tibet."

"Get some eyes on him. He might be useful in what we say to the public. Now, what are our options? Can we blow it up?"

"We're due downstairs for a briefing in three hours. Maybe we'll get some answers then."

The President turns to another, much younger man, Warren Bennett. "Warren, get me some TV time to address the nation. Come up with something I can say that'll prevent panic or civil unrest. Something that will keep folks from thinking the world's going to end."

The younger man nods brightly as he speaks, "We'll get on it right away. Funny, but I bet this helps us in the polls." Bennett stops when he sees the expression on the President and Bradshaw's faces.

"A war I can handle, Warren. Damn! Why'd this happen during my administration?"

. . .

Later, the various members of the National Security Council sit awaiting the President. As he enters the room the assembled visitors all stand. The President sits in his chair and the others take their seats. He looks at the man sitting behind a plaque identifying him as Robert Lewis, Secretary of Defense. "Okay. What have we got?"

Lewis turns to the scholarly-looking man on his right—it's Dr. Johansson. "I'm sure everyone has seen Dr. Johansson on the news. He's the foremost expert on rogue asteroids."

The President turns to Dr. Johansson. "How serious is this?"

"Mr. President, I should start off by showing you what we're dealing with. I understand that your own people have actual photographs of 2014 BD."

Secretary Lewis answers, "Uh, Mr. President, those images are from classified NRO assets."

The President looks at Lewis questioningly, "Didn't I see them on television?"

"No sir. Those were from the Hubble Telescope."

"Let's see 'em anyway. Doctor, keep it to yourself."

An image appears on the wall screen. It's the blackness of space with what looks like a rock in the center.

Dr. Johansson fights back a wave of nausea as his knees go weak. He stares at the image, *"...now I am become Death, the destroyer of worlds"*... the quote from the Bhagavad-Gita made famous by Oppenheimer upon seeing the first nuclear explosion in 1945 runs over and over in his head... *it's rock... my God... it's huge... breathe... get a grip...* "Oh, my." He pauses. "I... I was hoping it was mostly ice. But it's not. It appears to be rock." He continues to silently stare at the image.

The President looks at him questioningly, "Doctor?"

Johansson snaps out of it. "Sorry." He forces a smile. "Got sidetracked doing some quick calculations."

The President asks the question, "Is it going to hit us?"

"If there's no outside intervention, yes, it will collide with the earth on December 31st."

"How bad will it be?"

"The effects will be similar to a gigantic nuclear explosion, minus the radiation produced by a bomb. Earthquakes and tsunamis will be triggered and maybe some volcanic activity, too. The impact will also cause huge amounts of dust from the earth and the asteroid to erupt into the stratosphere and beyond."

"Like a nuclear winter?"

"Exactly like a nuclear winter. There will be months of total darkness and it will get very, very cold. There might even be changes in the earth's orbit after an impact of this magnitude."

The room falls silent for a moment as everyone digests this scenario.

The President is the first to speak. "Would anybody survive?"

"Maybe. If they survive the initial effects, have stores of food and water, and can survive the long period of intense cold. After that, we're just guessing."

The room falls quiet again.

"Can we blow the damned thing up?"

"Theoretically, yes. I mean, a nuclear explosion has always been our ace-in-the-hole for one that's this certain in a limited time frame."

The President nods. "Doctor, thanks for coming. We're going to consider your words very carefully. Please let us know if you have any further information or ideas about how to handle this situation. And it goes without saying, this is a matter of national security. We need to keep our conversation private. It stays inside this room."

"Of course."

"Good. We'll be in touch."

"Whatever I can do, Mr. President."

The President nods to an aide standing near the door. "Thomas will escort you out and arrange transportation for you. Thank you again."

Dr. Johansson shoves himself back from the table, turns and walks out with the aide. The door closes and the President turns to the Council. "I'm going on national television tonight and try to keep this thing from causing a mass panic. At some point within the next few days, I'm going to have to explain what it is we intend to do. I need options on the table by tomorrow afternoon."

DHARAMSALA

Tseten helps Angela and Jamie load their bags into a taxi as Samten Rinpoche and Chökli Rinpoche silently watch. Samten Rinpoche holds Jikme, who watches with wide eyes, while Chökli Rinpoche cradles a wrapped parcel in his arms.

Angela turns to the Rinpoches. "I'll send you a copy of the video just as soon as I've finished the editing. Your comments would be very helpful."

Samten Rinpoche smiles. "We look forward to seeing your work."

Jamie has been very quiet and Rinpoche has noticed. He turns to the boy. "I am very happy to have finally met you. You are indeed your father's son."

Jamie tries to smile as he replies, "It was nice to meet you."

"Do not be afraid of what you have discovered. I'm sure the coming months will offer great opportunities for us all." He places a hand on Jamie's shoulder. "Please take very good care of Lama Sang-Nagk's *gau*."

"I will."

Rinpoche nods to Chökli Rinpoche, who then steps toward Jamie and hands him the carefully wrapped package.

"For you."

Jamie gingerly takes the package from the Rinpoche. "What is it?"

Chökli Rinpoche gives Jamie one of his fierce looks that instantly turns into the broadest of smiles. "Take a look."

Jamie unwraps the red cloth, revealing an exact, hand painted, full-color copy of the black and white photograph of his father.

Angela is stunned. "Oh my God... it is so beautiful! Who did this?"

Samten Rinpoche smiles as he speaks, "Tseten is quite a good artist, don't you think?" Tseten, in embarrassment, silently looks down.

Jamie looks at the painting, then at Tseten. "Wow, dude... you did this? Thank you. Thank you so much."

"You are very welcome." Tseten smiles and starts the fist bang/tap/grab routine. Jamie laughs as they finish. Samten Rinpoche turns to Angela. "We will talk soon. Have a safe trip."

"Thank you so much. Let's go, Jamie."

Jamie turns to Tseten. "Take care of yourself. I'll e-mail you."

"Please keep me updated on your project."

"I will."

Angela and Jamie get into the taxi. As the vehicle pulls away from the monastery, Jamie looks out of the back window and waves. Through the window, we see the multicolored prayer flags fluttering in the breeze surrounding both Rinpoches and Tseten as they wave back, while Jikme just stares at the departing vehicle.

LAX INTERNATIONAL ARRIVAL TERMINAL

The US Customs Agent stares at his computer terminal for a long moment as Angela and Jamie stand with their bags. The agent takes their passports and stamps them both, saying "Welcome home" as he hands them to Angela.

"Thanks. Good to be back," Angela replies as she takes both passports and places them in her purse. She turns and points toward the door to their front. "That way, honey."

Angela and Jamie wheel their baggage through the door and then up a ramp into a crush of waiting humanity and the glare of bright lights.

An enthusiastic, young waiting woman reporter excitedly cries out, "There he is!" almost as if she had been on a whaler two centuries ago looking for the Great White. This is her moment and she's got her prey.

As Angela and Jamie step past the guards, the woman sticks a microphone in Jamie's face as a video cameraman jostles for position. "Jamie, how does it feel to have discovered how the world may end?"

Jamie looks exactly like a deer in the headlights. "Huh?"

"This is the most important thing that's ever happened! It's your discovery. How do you feel about it?"

Angela protectively moves in, "Excuse us, please." She grabs Jamie's hand and pushes her way through the other media people as she looks right and left... *my God, what a mob*... and then an older man in a straw hat, Hawaiian shirt and sunglasses suddenly appears—it's Ed.

He gives Angela a quick hug, then one for Jamie. "Couldn't get past these guys! Come on, I've got help out front."

The media aren't giving up. An older, slick-looking male reporter skillfully maneuvers in close and shoves his mike in Jamie's face as he says, "Jamie! Did you know everyone's calling your asteroid *Jamie's Rock*?"

A flicker of a smile crosses Jamie's face... *that's so cool!*... "No kidding?"

"Yep. It's *Jamie's Rock* now! Mrs. Edwards, can we set up an interview with Jamie?"

"Not right now."

"No problem. How about in a couple of hours?"

They've reached the curb and a van pulls up. Ed opens the door, shoves Jamie inside and slams the door closed. He and Angela go to the back of the vehicle and quickly load the baggage as the cameramen try to shoot Jamie through the van's tinted windows.

Another reporter jumps in, "Come on, Mrs. Edwards, give us a break."

Angela turns to the reporter, "Look, we've just spent thirty-six hours traveling and all of this is too much for him. Give us a chance to unpack, and then we'll talk it over with Jamie."

Several hands suddenly appear with business cards. Angela reluctantly takes them all and shoves them in a pocket. Then she and Ed get into the van, and they drive off, leaving the news crews in their wake.

WHITE HOUSE TELECONFERENCE ROOM

God, I should have had that drink... the President looks around the table. To his right, sitting with him in front of a TV camera, is Dr. Johansson... *good, right next to me where I can kick him if he goes off on a tangent...* and NASA director Eleanor Grenville to his left... *Eleanor's solid, she's all business all the time... too bad... good-looking woman....* Several staff—some in uniform—are seated around the room, out of the camera's view. One in particular catches his eye, General Albert Lewis, the Air Force Chief of Staff.

General Lewis is in full uniform, his left chest covered with the colorful ribbons and aviator wings of a man with a distinguished career in military aviation, a man who has risen to the top of his game. Beneath that carefully cultivated dignity lies what can only be described as a pained expression in his eyes. President Samuels looks at him, understanding his pain, ... *Christ, Al... I feel your pain, having to give up your secret toy to save the world...*

Eleanor looks at the series of large displays to her front. Somber looking heads of state peer down from the screens. Each screen is captioned with the appropriate nation's name: Russia, United Kingdom, France, China, India, Pakistan... *wonder why they didn't ask Israel, Japan, North Korea, or Brazil...? hell, everybody knows they have nukes...*

An aide motions to the President. He clears his throat as he speaks to the faces on the screens. "I'm going to turn this over to Dr. Edward Johansson, the world authority on rogue asteroids, and Dr. Eleanor Grenville, the director of NASA." He turns to his right. "Dr. Johansson, would you please tell us your findings?"

Dr. Johansson clears his throat... *showtime...* "Based on our analysis of the composition of 2014 BD, its velocity, and a few other considerations including potential margins of error, we've calculated that a thermonuclear device with the explosive power of sixty megatons will be required to destroy it. I'm told that such a device, or combination of devices, is available."

The President quietly notes the reaction of the heads of state—each reacts in their own way to the news that such large weapons still exist.

The French President is the first to speak, "I have been assured that we can have an Ariane ready for launch within three weeks."

Dr. Johansson looks to his left questioningly, and President Samuels smiles into the camera. "Thank you, Mr. President, but honestly, I worry about launching high-yield thermonuclear devices in unmanned rockets.

Especially when we don't have to." He turns to Eleanor, "Dr. Grenville, tell them what your folks came up with."

The Director of NASA is all business, "We'd prefer to load the devices in the cargo bay of the Orbital Space Plane, fly them up and dock with the International Space Station—"

The Indian President interrupts her. "Orbital Space Plane? Never heard of it. Are you going to bring a Space Shuttle out of retirement?"

President Samuels shakes his head, "No sir. We've been testing a crew transfer vehicle for some time now and were going to announce its existence in the near future anyway. I'm assured it's up to the job." The various faces on the screens try to maintain their deadpan expressions at this announcement.

The Russian President grimly smiles, "So... you've finally given it a name." President Samuels thinks ... *ah, Dimitri... did you really already know or are you just pretending that you knew?...* He glances at General Lewis, whose slightly raised eyebrows indicate that he, too, has noted the exchange.

The Indian President continues his questioning. "Now, are we to understand that you intend to assemble a delivery vehicle in orbit?"

Eleanor doesn't miss a beat, "Exactly. Plus, it'll make it a much simpler and more reliable vehicle if it doesn't have to stand the rigors of an earth launch through the atmosphere. Unmanned rockets will have previously rendezvoused the other components and fuel for the final stages. The astronauts will assemble the components, attach the devices to an in-flight guidance package and a terminal maneuvering unit, and join the whole thing to a propulsion module with enough fuel to do the job. It'll then be launched, and once it's in position, it'll be detonated."

The French President looks doubtful, "Do we have time for such a complex and ambitious undertaking?"

"We can be ready to launch in ninety days."

The Chinese Chairman also has doubts, "Very risky. Very complicated. And how will you secure the firing command?"

"Each device will have a separate and discrete code. All of the communications will be encrypted."

The British Prime Minister sits up and nods, "And you are looking for our participation."

President Samuels continues, "I don't want anyone to think that this has to be strictly an American project. We're talking about saving the earth. We all live here. And all of your countries have proven nuclear capabilities. The United States could do it alone but frankly, it seems more fitting for all of us to participate."

The Russian President finally speaks, "And of course, you would also like us to provide some of the nuclear devices?"

President Samuels' tone is ironic, "I'm told that each of us have some to spare."

The Russian continues, "Hmmm... I'm curious. Why were the other nuclear-capable nations not represented today?"

The President shrugs, "We understand that their weapons technology is not yet mature enough for this kind of an application." He turns to Eleanor, "Please, continue."

She speaks to the camera, "We'll want to assemble several separate devices, launch them in stages so if the first doesn't do what we want, then we have backups."

Dr. Johansson jumps in, "There's always the likely possibility that 2014 BD might disintegrate into fairly large pieces so we'll want to have some further options available."

The Chinese Chairman looks pleased with himself as he speaks, "I find it interesting that you want us to give you a nuclear weapon. If you remember, it was we who told the world these weapons might someday be used for precisely this purpose."

President Samuels nods as he speaks, "I'm sure you'll all want to consider what we've discussed here but please remember, we've got to make a decision within seven days. Anyone have anything to add?"

No one does.

"Well then, thank you all, and good-bye for now."

The screens flicker off, the camera is shut down and President Samuels reaches for the microphone on the table and flicks a switch back and forth. He nods at an aide, "Can you get rid of this? I've learned the hard way to make damned sure these things are really off."

He turns to Bradshaw, who observes, "Maybe the Russians and the Brits will play. The rest will be too nervous about letting us see what they've got."

Samuels grimly smiles and nods, "Yeah, I kind of figured that one out, too." He turns to Dr. Johansson and Eleanor as he picks up a TV remote and clicks a set on. "Let's see what's going on outside."

The screen comes to life. It's CNN, the news, and a replay of the clip of Jamie's homecoming at LAX. Jamie is surrounded by a crush of reporters, camera operators and the curious.

A reporter has a mike in Jamie's face as he speaks, "Jamie, how does it feel to have discovered how the world may end?"

Jamie looks stunned, "What do you mean?"

"This is the most important thing that's ever happened. It's your discovery. How do you feel about it?

"I don't know. I hope we can do something."

Angela suddenly comes into view, "Excuse us, please."

Dr. Johansson points to the screen, "That's his mother."

The President mutes the sound. "Where is he now?"

"At home, with his mother and grandfather."

The President continues to watch the now silent television image. "He's got a cool head—they didn't rattle him. Good. We can use him."

LOW EARTH ORBIT—MAY 6

The Orbital Space Plane, the sleeker, more curvaceous, and some might describe more ominous descendant of the Space Shuttle since it's original purpose was to be an orbital bomber, slowly approaches the International Space Station as it matches velocities.

Flying near the station is a "work area", which looks like a series of structural beams arranged in a framework to support lights, equipment, and four spidery craft. Three astronauts in space suits wave from within the structure. Attached to the structure is a banner that reads OPERATION EARTHSHIELD.

On the flight deck of the Orbital Space Plane, the flight commander glances out of his window and waves back.

"Those things look like big ol' bugs."

The pilot replies, "Looks ain't everything."

"Yeah, I ought to know." The commander keys his mike, "Charlie, you guys ready to get wet?"

Just a few feet behind the flight deck within the airlock, four space-suited figures hang on to restraints as they float in the confined space. Charlie looks around as he gives a thumbs-up—the three others return the gesture. Charlie nods. "We're good to go, boss."

"You're clear to vent the lock."

Charlie looks at one of the other astronauts and grins as his voice crackles over the comms.

"Man, I hate dumping good air; know what I mean?" He opens a control panel and turns a switch. There is a loud HISSISNG as the precious air vents into space... and then it's silent.

Against the star-speckled blackness of space, with a giant blue, white, and brown Earth as a backdrop, a hatch on the side of the Orbital Space Plane opens, and the astronauts float through, one by one, each tethered to the vehicle by a line. One of them opens another hatch and removes Manned Maneuvering Units (MMU), backpack devices each astronaut slides into that allow them to maneuver outside the space place.

They release their safety lines as the three waiting astronauts from the International Space Station arrive by way of their own MMUs.

Hans, one of the ISS astronauts slowly maneuvers toward Charlie. "Hey, what took you so long? That's twice as long as it took you in the pool."

"Yeah? Guess I was enjoying the view. You guys ready?"

"Let's do this."

The astronauts position themselves around the side of the space plane. Charlie waves toward the cockpit, "Okay, pop the goodie box."

After what seems like an interminable period, a hatch opens revealing within what appear to be three satellites. Each one is marked with a national flag of the providing nation: the United States, the Commonwealth of Independent States (Russia), and the United Kingdom. They are each also marked with the international radiation-warning symbol, revealing that this is no ordinary cargo.

. . .

The astronauts have released the weapons from the space plane. The three devices look innocent enough—dull, silver-colored cylinders that conceal massive, city-obliterating technological horrors. With the space plane and the earth in the background, one after another, each device is slowly guided by two astronauts toward the work area.

MALIBU HILLS, LOS ANGELES

The adobe styled house sits in the middle of a large, tree-covered field with a view of the ocean in the distance. A private security guard stands behind a wooden traffic barrier in the driveway. Several media vehicles are parked nearby.

In the living room, Angela and Ed watch the television as the feed from the space plane appears on the news. Ed shakes his head. "This gives me the creeps."

"Why?"

"Those are nuclear weapons in orbit around the earth. They're right over our heads. It was always a nightmare for my generation."

"That's ironic."

"How's that?"

"Weapons that could have destroyed the world may wind up saving it."

The telephone rings and a generic woman's voice answers the call. "Please leave your message at the tone." There's a beep and then, "Hi, this is Melissa Johnson at 'News of the Day'. Just checking in to see if you've reconsidered our offer. It would go a long way in helping to pay Jamie's college tuition, but we're open to discussion. We're here at (310) 853-1212 and we'd sure like to talk with you." The machine clicks off.

Ed and Angela look at each other. Angela shakes her head. "Maybe we ought to change our number."

"Maybe we ought to talk to them. Where's Jamie?"

"He's in his room."

. . .

Jamie's room is filled with pictures of astronomical objects and the earth from space, photos of space hardware, computers, a telescope, and posters of a couple of supermodels and rock music icons. A television showing the images of the Space Station activities has been muted and is being ignored. Next to his bed is a small Tibetan Buddhist shrine with an image of Avalokiteshvara, and the painting of his father prominently placed in the center.

Jamie sits on his bed. He's writing in a notebook and referring to a thick Tibetan-English dictionary. His fingers skillfully copy a line of Tibetan characters into the notebook, and his calligraphy has greatly improved from the near-scribbles seen before.

Tycho comes into the room and drops his head on Jamie's leg. Jamie rolls over and absently begins to scratch the dog's head as he stares at the ceiling—it's covered with images of stars, planets and galaxies. He pulls the *gau* out of his shirt and holds it. Tycho nuzzles his hand.

"Hey, come on… you can't eat it." Jamie rolls over on his stomach. "Want to see it?" He starts to open it, then pauses. "I better not." He glances at the television, picks up the remote and turns up the volume.

Chapter 3

DROLMA

MOUNTAIN RIDGE, INDO-TIBETAN BORDER

The blazing sun beams down through a crystal clear blue sky onto the dazzling white snow-covered mountains below. A beautiful, full-grown snow leopard slowly walks across an open snowfield. He stops for a moment to sniff the brisk air. The creature is magnificent.

. . .

A drawn bowstring nestles to the side of a nut-brown, weathered face, just below its squinting right eye. The eye narrows down almost to a slit. The bowstring is released with a *sshoomp*!

The snow leopard's ears alert at the sound. He starts to turn his head as the arrow *smacks* on his right rear hindquarter, the blunt, rounded tip bouncing off of the animal. He snarls and jumps with pain.

BANG! A plume of snow kicks up where the animal was just a moment ago. The snow leopard takes off in a dead run and leaps over a nearby ridge.

. . .

The American hunter and his local guide, Apho, are both dressed in white camouflage. The hunter is furious and screams in his east-coast accent, "Son-of-a-fucking-bitch!"

Apho turns his binoculars to his left. Through the eyepieces, he sees that the bowman, in reality, is a bow-woman.

Tu-Chen Mo, clad in her own white rag camouflage, defiantly stands and whips the white cloth wrap off of her head. She is an imposing figure, mid-forties (who can tell?), long black hair and powerfully built. She's beautiful, but looks a lot like a Mongol warrior, and even more like the "warrior woman" Jamie and Angela saw where Lama Sang-Nagk died.

Tu-Chen Mo angrily shakes her bow in Apho's direction and hurls her angry words in Tibetan, *"Apho, you piece of yak shit! You sell your skills to this fat butcher and hunt the beautiful cat! Lord Yama will eat your guts in each of the six hells!"*

The hunter takes his hat off and angrily throws it on the snow. "By God, for fifteen thousand dollars I am going to shoot me something!" In a cold fury, he swings his rifle toward Tu-Chen Mo and takes aim.

Apho's eyes almost pop out of their sockets. He shoves the rifle off target. *BANG!* The rifle fires into the air.

WHACK! A blunt arrow hits the hunter on the arm.

"Shit!" The hunter drops the rifle, clutches his arm in pain, and turns to Apho. "What the hell'd you do that for?!"

"Ai-yah!! You do not understand! That is Tu-Chen Mo! She protects the creatures of these mountains. It is the most terrible karma if you kill her!"

"Karma my ass! What about my leopard? I gotta' leave tomorrow!"

Apho picks up the rifle and hat. His face is thoughtful as he knocks the snow off the hat and hands it back to the hunter. "Maybe next time Tu-Chen Mo stays home."

The hunter snatches his hat and slams it on his head. "Next time?   And another fifteen-thousand fucking dollars?"

Apho has already turned and is walking away, the rifle slung on his shoulder. The hunter starts to walk after him. "Hey, Apho! I'm talking to you!"

Tu-Chen Mo stands watching the hunter and Apho in the distance as they walk down the mountain. She shakes her head in disgust, then turns and glances up toward the next ridge.

The snow leopard stands, his tail swishing back and forth, looking down at Tu-Chen Mo. He makes low *ruf-rufing* sounds.

Tu-Chen Mo squints up through the glare at the animal. *"Kan-Seek! Pay attention next time! I can't be everywhere!"*

. . .

It's a long walk, but if you come down from the mountains and you know where to look, there are lovely forests. Tu-Chen Mo walks through them with the ease of someone completely at home, her bow slung across her chest. As she reaches a clearing, she pauses and looks up at two birds circling just above the trees.

She reaches into a pouch and her strong hand comes out with some grain. She pours half into her other hand, then holds her arms out to her sides as if in prayer, palms up.

The two birds swoop down and land on her outstretched arms, nibble at the grain, then walk up to her shoulders and perch. Tu-Chen Mo's voice is gentle, *"What? No song for me?"*

The birds begin to sing to her and to each other for several minutes, and then they fly off.

Tu-Chen Mo watches them fly away as she laughs with delight, *"That will certainly do!"*

LEH, LADAKH

Tu-Chen Mo is herself a colorful figure as she walks past the small shops, stores and inns, and makes her way through the walking inhabitants of Leh: local Indians, Tibetans, Buddhist monks, and western tourists and trekkers. She carries a large bundle on her back worn like a pack. A few of the locals acknowledge her presence with the traditional palms pressed together at the heart, accompanied by a slight bow of the head. She returns the greetings with a smile, sometimes a word or two.

She stops at a store, then enters into a main room packed from floor to ceiling with an eclectic variety of goods: Indian, Chinese and a few American canned foods, clothing, postcards, shoes, religious articles, blankets, infant care items, DVDs, magazines, etc. Several tourists are looking at various items as the store owner, a stout, short man in a white shirt and traditional baggy trousers, a couple of Buddhist rosaries—*malas*—around his neck and several intricate bracelets on his thick wrists, answers questions.

The tourists glance at this dusty, interesting looking woman, then go back to their browsing.

The storeowner's face breaks into a huge smile as he greets her in Tibetan. *"Tu-Chen Mo! An auspicious arrival! I have no more of your wonderful prayer wheels and these visitors are looking for something magnificent!"*

Tu-Chen Mo barely smiles as she slips out of the heavy bundle and hands it to the owner, who in turn gives it to an assistant. This time he speaks in English, making sure the customers can hear his praise. "Show these to our customers. They are the finest to be found, carved by our friend, Tu-Chen Mo." He switches back to Tibetan as he speaks to Tu-Chen Mo, *"There is someone waiting for you. Because of you, Tu-Chen Mo, I am most honored that he has stayed with us. Come."*

The store owner turns and leads Tu-Chen Mo to the back of the store and the stairs.

The owner's assistant reaches into the bundle and removes a carved wooden prayer wheel. He places it in the hands of a British tourist and gives it a spin. "We believe that when the wheel spins, its prayer goes out into the world."

The tourist runs his hand over the wood. "Good heavens, Martha. Look at this." The man's wife turns and examines the prayer wheel. The Tibetan lettering on the wheel is the same as Jamie's attempts, only much finer, and has been carved in relief. The wood has been polished to a rich color, the characters almost glowing with an inner luminosity.

The woman tentatively touches it, "It's exquisite." She spins the wheel. It rotates as if it were built with the finest bearings. "We simply must have it." The clerk smiles.

Upstairs, Tu-Chen Mo and the storeowner are now barefoot. The tapestried door hanging is pushed aside and the storeowner holds it open for his guest.

Daylight streams in through several windows. The floor of the room is covered with colorfully woven rugs. There is a Buddhist shrine along one wall. A flat screen TV and DVD player sit in the middle of another.

A children's cartoon plays as Chökli Rinpoche, one arm wrapped around the small child sitting next to him on the floor, both intently watch the screen. They are lost in the action with wide smiles, but the Rinpoche's lips continue to silently mouth his mantras as the beads from his *mala* make their way under his thumb.

As Tu-Chen Mo walks into the room, Rinpoche turns and faces the door. The sight of this fierce, old man with the small child, both watching cartoons, almost brings a smile to her face. Instead, it's the old Rinpoche's face that splits into a huge smile as he brings his hands up in greeting, the *mala* hanging down between his palms. *"It is good to see you."*

Tu-Chen Mo returns the greeting in a sign of respect, and a bit of resignation... *this can't be good....* She remains standing in the doorway.

Chökli Rinpoche motions for her to enter, *"Please, come in."*

She enters the room and sits on a cushion facing the old man. Chökli Rinpoche whispers in the boy's ear and the child silently mutes the sound and then stands and leaves the room. Rinpoche smiles again. *"You look wonderful, like a bandit from long ago. Or a sorceress!"*

She shrugs. *"I have no mirror. And as a wise Lama once told me, one can never actually see one's own face."* She pauses for a moment, *"I believe those were your words."*

Chökli Rinpoche chuckles at the memory. *"I hear the most wonderful stories about you. Stories about you and your animal friends, how you can call the elements, even stories that you can fly!"*

"Really. And you believe them?"

"You've spent many years alone in the mountains. You always were a most skilled yogini. Nothing you might attain would surprise me."

There's no reaction to the Rinpoche's words. She just sits and continues to gaze at him.

He continues. *"I've always suspected that this was exactly what you were meant to do."*

"Please, forgive me, and I don't mean to be rude but I have a very long walk home. You, too, have come a long way. May I ask what is it you wished to discuss?"

Rinpoche nods, taking no offense. *"Did you know your brother, Lama Sang-Nagk, had passed?"*

She barely nods. *"Yes. This world is much diminished with his passing."*

"And how did you know of this?"

"No matter the distance, he was always with me and I, with him."

"Did you know he achieved 'jalü', the rainbow body?"

Tu-Chen Mo closes her eyes for a moment. When she opens them, they are moist. *"Would you have expected less? My brother was the kindest, most compassionate being I have ever known."*

Both sit silently for a long moment, and then she speaks. *"But you are here because of the wheel. Korlo Gön-Poy has stopped."*

"Of course, I have not seen that with my own eyes. Yet you already know this. Have you been there?"

"No, but I have 'seen' it."

Chökli Rinpoche nods. *"Do you also know of the heavenly body that will collide with the earth two months before Losar?"*

Tu-Chen Mo looks surprised. "Others know of this?"

Rinpoche smiles. *"Only the entire world."*

"I come here only a few times a year. I rarely speak with anyone."

Rinpoche nods, *"They tell us the collision will surely mean the end of this world."*

Tu-Chen Mo shrugs, *"Not if Sang-Nagk's most senior empowered disciple performs the ritual and restarts it."*

Rinpoche shakes his head, *"Sadly, there is no one left."*

Tu-Chen Mo's head snaps up, *"That cannot be!"*

Rinpoche continues, *"There have been many deaths recently. The invaders captured his senior student only three months ago. Lama Sang-Nagk had only just begun with another, and he has also died."*

"Then this world is truly finished...," she observes sadly, *"... and frankly, I'm surprised it took so long."*

The old man reaches for a pot of tea and a cup. *"Would you like some tea?"*

"Thank you."

Rinpoche pours them both a cup. Tu-Chen Mo noisily slurps from hers. He looks at her over his cup, *"You, alone, now know the ritual."*

There's a bitterness as she speaks, *"And I am no longer worthy to perform it. I can thank the invaders for opening my eyes to my own faults."*

Rinpoche's words are gentle. *"Please, it was an act of courage to save others. And for such a being as you, under the circumstances, it was the only choice you could possibly have made."*

Her eyes are downcast as she speaks, *"We learn from the teachings that the only constant is impermanence... change is the only thing that never changes. We know in our hearts that with time, all things will change. But, Rinpoche, even after all of these years, we are still being tortured and murdered. Our language, our culture, our very nature is being deliberately destroyed as if the invaders wish that we would simply turn to dust, to be blown away by the wind, to disappear as if our feet had never walked this land for more than a thousand years. The very land itself is being corrupted, destroyed, and now, out of desperation, our people are burning themselves—they are actually setting themselves on fire, hoping that such a horrific and public sacrifice will cause the world to learn of our suffering and injustice.*"

She pauses for a long moment, then shakes her head in wonder, "*I find it almost funny that the most important gift we have, our wisdom culture, that which could be used to solve all of the problems facing this world, is that which they most want to destroy. There were times when I thought I should just join them in a flaming death. Now, it seems that is a decision events have made for me.*"

She pauses for a moment, silently shaking her head. "*Of what use am I when I am so unworthy? But it doesn't seem to really matter now, does it?*"

They sit in silence for a long moment, and when Rinpoche speaks, his voice is a soft whisper, "*Will you not at least try?*"

Her downturned face slowly shakes from side to side. Her despair hangs on her, like a weight pressing her down. *"I do not know if it's even possible now."*

The old man's voice is very gentle, *"One's karma is often like one's face. As you said, you can never really see it for yourself. But dear one, I see you and you are most certainly worthy, regardless of what you may think. Many, many others have felt the same way for years. We've respected your wish for privacy, patiently waiting for the day when you would return to us. And now, somewhere inside, you must know, because you are worthy, that this task is possible."*

Tu-Chen Mo sits as if it takes some time for the words to sink in. *"What of the prayer of Tokden-Ö-Zel?"*

"I know where it is."

She turns and gazes at the *thangka* of Padmasambhava over the shrine for some time. *"Then I must have it if I am to even try."*

Rinpoche brings his hands up to the image of Padmasambhava and nods a silent prayer of thanks. *"As Lama Sang-Nagk was dying, he gave it to a boy."*

She looks up as if not believing what she has just heard. *"What? A boy? What boy?"*

The old man reaches into his robe and brings out a color photograph and hands it to her.

She squints as she looks at the photograph of Angela and Jamie. *"Surely these two were not on Gönpoy-Ri!"*

"No. Lama Sang-Nagk had come down from the mountain."

This news electrifies her.

"Do you know what this means? This boy, is he a monk? He doesn't look like a monk. Has he even had any instruction?"

Rinpoche barely shrugs, *"His father gave him some instruction in meditation."*

Where is he from? Is he English, German?"

"American. In fact, it is he who discovered the heavenly object that threatens to destroy us all."

Confusion crosses her face as she speaks, *"I don't understand. What do you mean 'it is he who discovered it'?"*

"The boy is something of a prodigy. He studies astronomy."

Tu-Chen Mo's interest heightens. *"Really? Does he know of the 'pel-doong's' importance?"*

"He knows it is important. He does not know why. He knows how to care for it. The woman—his mother—is sympathetic to our people's situation."

Tu-Chen Mo looks very tired as she silently considers what she's heard. Her eyes close as she tries to settle her own thoughts. When she finally speaks, it's with a great deal of resignation. *"This ritual is like no other. It takes a very special practitioner to accomplish all that is required. His or her heart must be so pure that it is their first nature to put all others before oneself because really, that is the only source of the power that is required for its successful completion. Anything less could easily result in not only failure, but the destruction of the one attempting to facilitate the ritual. It takes years, decades of intense practice to develop that kind of purity and precious few ever attain that level."*

Rinpoche looks at her, confusion fills his eyes. *"I thought <u>you</u> were to perform the ritual."*

"Sang-Nagk gave the 'pel-doong' to the boy for a reason. If <u>I</u> were destined to perform the ritual, he would have given it to me."

"Would it make any difference if I told you that the boy's father was Jake Edwards?"

The words hit her with a force that she cannot quite conceal as she speaks, *"Jake Edwards is his father?"*

"Yes."

"And the boy is the one who first discovered the coming catastrophe?" She pauses for a long moment. *"Sang-Nagk deliberately chose him, and yet, he is truly untrained by any remote measure of our tradition."* There's another long pause. *"Then you must send him to me."*

It's all Rinpoche can do to keep from smiling as he thinks... *yes!... Drolma... you're still here... and you've returned to fulfill your karma... your destiny...*

Tu-Chen Mo sits up a little, not much, but there's a shift as if she has become infused with power, the power of purpose... a reason to be. She looks directly into Rinpoche's eyes, *"You must send him to me. Only then can I determine if this is at all possible."*

"Can you not come to Dharamsala with me and meet with him there?"

"What must be done is better done here."

"When do you want to see him?"

"I will send a message to the storeowner when I am ready." She pauses for a moment. *"The woman, his mother, she should come, too."*

She reaches for the old man's hands with hers. She takes them by the fingers, leans forward, and touches them to her own forehead. Then she stands.

He looks up at her. *"Drolma Pa-Mo, why have you taken a secular name?"*

"It is sacrilege to continue to use the sacred name that was given me."

Rinpoche's face is kindness itself. *"Dear child, no one deserves it more than you. Those who knew you will always remember you as Drolma Pa-Mo. May we again know you this way?"*

She nods, *"As you wish."*

"Good. Oh, there is one more thing. Jake Edwards." He pauses before continuing. *"He may have returned."* He hands her another, smaller photo. *"There were rumors, I went with others to investigate the possibility of a 'tulku', and it was then that we... well..."*

Drolma looks at the photos. She stares motionlessly at Rinpoche for a long moment. Then, tucking the photos inside her tunic, she turns and exits the room.

Chökli Rinpoche sits in silence. He looks at the cartoon show still silently running on the TV. Then he turns to the shrine and returns to his practice.

Chapter 4

OBSTACLES

NASA COMPUTER FACILITY

Tim Gordon, PhD, is kind of a teddy bear of a man. Late forties, a nicely trimmed beard, glasses, carrying a little extra weight, he sits at a computer workstation with Air Force Colonel Jesse Lincoln. Gordon taps on the keyboard and the two men watch as lines of code slowly scroll down the screen. Tim nods approvingly. "Looks good to me, Colonel. I think you've got it covered."

"I damn well better. We'll look like idiots if they don't go bang."

"Only until the end of the year."

"Now there's a cheerful thought."

Tim smiles and removes the flash drive from the computer. Emblazoned on the drive are the words TOP

SECRET–EARTHSHIELD FIRING CODES. Tim hands the drive to the Colonel, who slips it into a metal case, and then locks it inside a safe. He signs the safe register as he speaks.

"Don't want that little puppy getting out."

"No kidding."

"Okay, thanks, Tim. I think we're set. See you at the staff meeting."

"You betcha'."

Colonel Lincoln exits the room. Tim waits for a moment and then picks up the iPhone and headphones that were lying on the table next to the monitor. He unclips a tiny, almost invisible wire from the device and removes the other from the rear of the monitor. He taps a few times on the iPhone's screen, puts on his headphones, stands and exits the room.

In the outer office, Tim stops at the guard station to sign out. The guard smiles as he asks, "What'cha' listening to today?"

"The Resurrection Gospel Singers latest—'It's The End of The World'."

"You gotta be kidding! Hey, let me give you one of my playlists!"

"You're funny. You know very well that head-banger stuff you listen to would blow my eyeballs right out of their sockets."

"C'm on, doc, you might like it."

Tim laughs. "Yeah, right. Good night, pal." He shakes his head as he walks away down the hall.

NASA MISSION CONTROL, HOUSTON— JUNE 2

Above the activity on the floor, high up in the glassed-in VIP section overlooking mission control, Jamie and Ed (both looking dapper in suits and ties), and Angela in a classy blue suit of her own, sit with a number of civilian dignitaries from several countries and their NASA escorts. As Ed takes in the surroundings, Jamie is totally absorbed in writing in a notebook. Angela glances down at it. "Why do you keep writing that?"

Jamie shrugs, never looking up. "I don't know. I like doing it."

"Put it away. It's time."

There's a commotion in the back of the room, and then the President and his entourage enters. The President strides down to where Jamie is now standing. He sticks out his hand with a big smile. "Jamie Edwards. What a pleasure."

Jamie shakes the President's hand. "Hi, Mr. President."

The President turns to Angela and Ed. "You've raised a fine young man."

Angela beams. "We like him."

The President laughs as he turns to Bennett. "Warren, where would you like us?"

"Sir, if you'd all come with me over to the table, we'll start. We're right on schedule."

Several minutes later, the president stands alongside Jamie in front of a television camera. Angela and Ed stand just behind Jamie, both of them calmly trying to contain their excitement as their eyes are riveted on the large screen to their front, showing a live image of the four spacecraft.

On cue, the President begins. "Hello to you all. Above us, orbiting our beautiful and precious planet, are four spacecraft."

. . .

In a rural village in India, a gathering of villagers sits outside on the ground in front of a television set as they watch the President's address under a night sky. On the screen, the President continues.

"These spacecraft have been constructed by a multinational team in a spirit of world-wide cooperation. It is now time to send them on their way, so that our many different peoples can live to fulfill their dreams and destinies."

A little boy stares up into the night sky, a worried look on his young face. His mother protectively wraps an arm around him.

. . .

Inside a bar in a *favela* in Rio de Janeiro, several patrons sit staring at the television over their glasses of beer.

"The leaders of these countries and I unanimously agreed that the choice for who would launch these spacecraft should be someone who symbolizes the hopes and dreams of us all, the young man who first alerted the world to this threat, Jamie Edwards."

The President turns to Angela and Ed.

"With him is his mother, Angela Edwards, and his grandfather, Ed Edwards."

One of the men watching nods appreciatively as he says, *"Ay! The mother is good looking."*

The woman sitting next to him punches the man on the arm, *"Why are you always looking? You are a pig!"*

. . .

The President turns to Jamie and motions to a box on a platform. A large, internally lighted red push-button shines on top.

"Jamie, it's time to launch the EARTHSHIELD rockets. Five, four, three, two, one, NOW!"

Jamie presses the button, and it turns from red to green. The President nods in approval. "God speed. Now, let's watch that large screen down front."

. . .

Near the International Space Station, the four spacecraft are now parked outside the construction structure. Three are identical while the fourth bristles with various kinds of antennae. Several astronauts in space suits and MMUs wait near the space station. One of them holds a television camera, focusing on one of the spacecraft as a small plume of blue flame shoots out of the rear of the spidery craft. Silently and slowly, it begins to accelerate as it moves away from the others, picking up speed, and quickly disappears into the blackness of space.

The camera switches to the second spacecraft and it, too, begins to move, accelerate, and then disappears from view.

Inside the ISS, Hans watches the last vehicle as it disappears into space. He looks over at one of his team members and wonders out loud what they all might be thinking, "You ever think we'd be better off up here if all of this doesn't work?"

. . .

Inside the monastery office in Dharamsala, Chökli Rinpoche, Samten Rinpoche and several others sit in front of a large computer screen, watching the pictures from orbit. To one side sit Tseten and Jikme. The little boy's total attention is focused on the images, as Tseten gently strokes the boy's hair. Everyone except for the child works their *mala* beads in one hand as they silently say their prayers.

. . .

Near the International Space Station, the fourth and last spacecraft is beginning to move and then accelerates. The astronauts silently clap their space-suited hands and hold "thumbs up" as it disappears from view.

LOS ANGELES

On the stage at a television studio, Jamie sits with Regina Landis of *The Regina Landis Show*, broadcasting live with a packed audience. Regina, one of those sincere and totally upbeat personalities who can just make it all better by simply flashing her perfect and sincere smile is taking questions directed to Jamie. "Yes ma'am. The pretty lady in blue."

An assistant holds a microphone for an older woman in the audience as she stands. "What were you doing in Tibet?"

"My mom was making a film about how the people are suffering under the Chinese and how they're losing their culture."

Regina turns to Jamie, "What do you think about that?"

"It's really sad. They've got amazing art and the people are really nice."

Regina looks out into the audience. "Yes, sir. You with the Lakers jacket."

A lanky young man stands and asks, "You think those rockets are gonna' do any good?"

Jamie's face brightens, "Sure. NASA's really good at this stuff. They're going to hit the asteroid and blow it up." The audience cheers and applauds

Regina looks at Jamie with that huge smile, "Well, you've got a lot of confidence!"

"It's just good science and engineering."

Regina points to the audience again. "Yes ma'am."

A younger woman with features showing the signs of strain, bends toward the microphone in front of her. "Don't you wish you'd never seen this thing?"

"Huh?"

"I mean, what if it doesn't work? Maybe you're too young to remember when the Challenger and Columbia blew up, but sometimes they make mistakes. And I've heard that it could break into smaller parts that could still kill us all. Maybe it would have been better to just never have known..." Her voice trails off as she begins to cry. "I mean, I'm so scared..." The woman completely breaks down into wracking sobs, and the audience is dead silent. Jamie has that deer-in-the-headlights look again.

Regina comes to the rescue. "Well honey, it's okay. We're all a little scared but we've got to have faith that God still has plans for each and every one of us. Personally, I think we're going to be just fine. Okay, let's take a break and we'll be right back!" The music cues up, Regina holds her smile for a moment, and then she turns to Jamie. "How're you feeling, sweetheart?"

"She makes it sound like it's my fault," as he unconsciously rubs the inside of his left forearm through his jacket.

Regina gives Jamie a big hug, "Well, it's not. You're doing great! Don't worry, sugar. We'll have 'em all laughing again."

Jamie gives a half smile as Regina turns to talk to one of the staff, still rubbing the inside of his forearm.

. . .

While Jamie reaches into his school locker, looking for a book, he glances a few lockers down the hall and sees Slammer and a couple of his crew. Slammer looks at Jamie and something catches his eye. "Well shit, check it out." He saunters up to Jamie. "Lemme see your ink."

Jamie looks at him blankly. "Huh?"

Slammer starts to grab Jamie's left arm, but Jamie catches his hand, and that catches Slammer by surprise. "Hey, whassup little man? Don't get all weird on me now. Just want to see your tattoo. Gotta be new. Wasn't there before."

Jamie stares into Slammer's eyes for a long moment, then slowly pushes up his sleeve, revealing the dark blue Tibetan characters on his skin. Slammer's eyes widen as he examines the quality and fineness of the markings. "Damn, little bro', that's some fine shit. Detailed." He laughs. "What'd you do, go sign up at some Kung-Fu place? You been takin' Kung-Fu so you can kick my ass?" He and his friends laugh. "It's Chinese, right? So you got inked up over there?"

Jamie slowly rolls his sleeve down. "It's not a tattoo."

Slammer laughs again and looks at his posse. "It's not a tattoo, yeah, right." He turns back to Jamie with a sarcastic, "Uh huh. It just got there all by itself. What's it mean, name of the Kung-Fu place?"

"It's Tibetan—'om jeek-tin dee kyohb hoong'."

Slammer looks at Jamie as if he's speaking... well, Tibetan. "Now that sure don't tell me shit at all. What's it mean in American?"

Principal Jackson approaches the boys. "Jamie, Winston, the rest of you, shouldn't you gentlemen be getting to class?"

"It's Slammer," mutters Winston/Slammer as he turns in disgust and walks away.

Principal Jackson shakes his head as he watches Slammer and the others saunter down the hall. "Everything okay, Jamie?"

Jamie looks up, and nods. "Yes sir. We're cool."

"How are things at home?"

"Everything's good, sir. Thanks for asking. I better get going." Jamie turns and heads down the hall, leaving Principal Jackson watching as he disappears around a corner.

. . .

Angela sits in front of her computer, staring at the image of Avalokiteshvara, touching up a pixel here, blending in a color there, totally lost in the moment. She pauses, sensing something, or more accurately, sensing nothing... *it sure is quiet...*

She pushes back from the desk, stands, and walks out of the room.

In the living room, Ed is asleep in front of the muted television. Angela enters and sits on the sofa. She picks up the remote and begins to click through the channels, pausing when an image of rural Idaho appears. She turns up the volume.

On the screen, Kathy, an interviewer, is questioning a heavyset, middle-aged man, Brother LeRoy, as they stand outside what is obviously a gussied-up, triple-wide mobile home. In the background, several other home sites are visible. Most have a flagpole with an American flag hanging still in the heat.

"So, Brother LeRoy, you don't give 'Operation EarthShield' much of a chance."

Brother LeRoy is a friendly, charismatic man with an easy way about him, but he radiates an intensity that is first revealed by his eyes... they're a little pinched, and he's wound just a little too tightly.

"You know, Kathy, all the signs point for those who would see that these are indeed the end times. God has had enough of man's evil ways; the corruption, immorality, pollution, the blasphemy. I believe the good Lord is going to weed this garden. Our puny attempts to avoid the coming apocalypse aren't going to alter His master plan one little bit."

"'EarthShield' is still on course."

"Well, the fat lady hasn't sung yet, has she?"

"You really think it's the end of the world?"

"It's most certainly the end of *your* world. However, we here at Resurrection's Eden will most surely survive. We've heeded our own advice, and we're prepared for any eventuality. In fact, let me show you some of the survival items we can provide to your viewers—"

Angela clicks to another channel. A talk show is in progress and LaTasha and Jason are sitting onstage. Marsha, the show's host, turns to the woman. "Now LaTasha, what do you think is the real problem?"

"The problem is that this dope thinks just because HE thinks we all gonna die in December that he can just {BLEEP} around all he wants 'cause it don't matter no how."

Jason, the dope in question, silently shakes his head and rolls his eyes.

Marsha turns to him. "Jason, you don't think those rockets are going to work? Honey, they've got atomic bombs on them."

"Hell no, they ain't gonna work." The audience BOOS. "I mean, c'm on, that thang's a asteroid big as *Deeetroit*. No way they gonna stop it. So what the hell, why not do everthang? Ain't gonna matter no how."

Marsha shakes her head as she speaks. "Jason, you've got yourself one cheerful outlook on life." She fires off her thousand-watt version of "the smile" to the camera. "Okay, we've got to take a break and then we'll be right back with someone who says it's all a secret plot by the government to get everybody under a one-world government. Wonder if that's all the same government? Stay with us!"

Angela changes the channel. It's a local news program. The anchor continues, "… so let's go to Maria Chavez in Canoga Park." The scene switches to a residential street that, even with the media trucks, is strangely quiet. A reporter stands in front of a yellow-taped house where coroner personnel are wheeling out gurneys with bodies.

The reporter begins, "Steve, neighbors tell us Mrs. Altoonian believed that 'Jamie's Rock', the huge asteroid that's on a collision course with the earth, will never be stopped. Apparently, she was so distraught that she gathered her family together, shot them, and then shot herself. There still needs to be—"

Angela clicks the television off and leaves the room. She pauses at the hallway, then turns down toward Jamie's room, stops at the door, and listens for a moment—there's no sound. She taps on the door.

"Jamie?" There's no answer. She glances at her watch, then taps a little louder.

"Jamie? It's only eight. You're not asleep already, are you?" Still no answer.

"Jamie? Are you all right?" Silence. Angela turns the doorknob and opens the door.

The room is barely lit by the small desk lamp. The walls and ceiling are covered with the Tibetan characters. Even the pictures and posters are covered with the calligraphy.

Jamie, facing the wall and wearing only shorts, stands at the last bit of empty wall space, a marker in his hand. His body is covered with... something. He turns and smiles.

"Hi, Mom."

He begins to draw the characters faster than the eyes can follow. His hand moves in a blur as a six-by-three foot expanse of wall is quickly filled with precise, perfectly constructed lines of Tibetan calligraphy, each line exactly like the one before it, all exactly as seen on the carving.

Angela turns on the overhead light. Jamie turns around, revealing the lines of Tibetan characters that are all over his body.

She cries out, "Oh my God!"

Jamie grasps the *gau* around his neck as, with a fearlessly calm curiosity, he examines the characters on his arm.

"I'm changing, Mom, but it's okay." Just then, Jamie's eyes are caught by something outside the window. He stares through the glass—it's Drolma, outside, flanked by two snow leopards, staring back at him. "Mom! She's here!"

. . .

Later that night, Angela sits at the dining room table as she flips through a thick Tibetan-English dictionary.

Ed walks in and heavily sits. "He's asleep. We could take him to the hospital—"

Angela's head snaps up. "Are you kidding? They'd put him in a psychiatric ward."

"Honey, why would he have somebody paint him up like that? They're even in the middle of his back."

"Nobody painted him."

"Oh come on, Angela. He couldn't do it by himself."

"And I'm telling you it's not paint or tattoos or anything like that. Dammit, I looked at them with a magnifying glass."

"Well what the hell are they then?"

"I think they just… appeared."

"They just appeared, huh?" Ed shakes his head, "Hell, maybe it's witchcraft. He's still got that thing around his neck."

"He's supposed to take care of it and he doesn't want to take it off."

"Yeah? Well maybe he oughta!" Ed glances at the dictionary. "You figure out what it says?"

"I think it's some kind of prayer."

"Look, what do you want to do? What's going to happen when he goes to school like that? They're going to call you, then they'll call Child Protective Services—"

"He's not going back to school. He says he doesn't feel sick, he doesn't have a fever, he seems calm, accepting of it. I don't know what to do." She closes her eyes for a moment and takes a breath. "Nobody here is going to have a clue about any of this. And Jamie said the woman was here—he insists he saw her."

"We both checked! There was no one there!"

"Maybe we need to go back."

"Back? Back where?"

"India. To Samten Rinpoche."

Ed sits for a long moment. "Yeah, well, if you're going, I'm going with you."

The two of them sit for a long moment, listening to the wind rising outside. There's a strange, foreign quality to the sound, as if the wind were coming from somewhere else, as if it didn't really belong here, touching these trees for the very first time. Ed stands and walks back into the hallway.

Jamie's room is again lit only by the soft light of his desk lamp. He's tucked in his bed, asleep, as the door quietly opens and Ed enters. Ed slowly walks over to the bed and kneels down next to the sleeping boy. He looks at Jamie for a long moment, then reaches for the *gau* sitting on the boy's softly rising chest. His hand is almost touching it when Jamie's eyes open and his own hand protectively grasps the *gau*. Ed's hand freezes.

"Hi Grandpa."

"Hey tiger. Didn't mean to wake you."

"It's okay." He looks down at the *gau*. "They told me no one should touch it except me."

Ed brings his hand down with resignation and sits on the bed. "After we lost your Dad, I swore an oath to take care of you, no matter what it took." Tears well up as he continues. "All of this stuff scares the crap out of me, Jamie. I'm so afraid for you. I love you so much. I... I can't stand the thought of losing you, too."

Jamie sits up and takes Ed's hand in his own. "It's okay, Grandpa. It's going to be okay." He looks at Ed. "Mom and I are going to have to go back, aren't we?"

"Looks like it. And dammit, this time I'm going with you!"

Jamie smiles. "That'll be cool. You're going to love it. No beach though."

Ed listens for a moment to the rising wind. "Oh, yeah. I can hardly wait."

INDO-TIBETAN MOUNTAIN FOREST

A lone figure is visible in a snow-covered clearing among the trees, surrounded by snow-white mountains visible through the crystal clear night.

Drolma sits on a sheepskin, legs and feet crossed in lotus, her hands on her knees. She wears only a thin cotton shirt and trousers. Her thick, black hair hangs down around her face and shoulders, flecked with flakes of snow. Her breath is a visible thick cloud of fog in the intense cold of the night air.

As she sits, she sings a low, sweet chant as her eyes look up at the mountaintops. An almost invisibly faint mist begins to rise from her body. Her hands move gracefully as they form the *mudras* of the ritual. The chanting has no beginning and no end... it just continues.

Around her, almost too slowly to see happen, the snow on the ground begins to melt in a circle that inches out away from her. As she continues to chant, the dark ground becomes visible, and Drolma looks to be on an island in a white sea. The heat radiating from her body turns the melted snow into vapor, and its tendrils gently swirl around her, at times almost masking her from view.

Her voice trails off into silence. Like an unseen drum, distant rolling thunder sounds, its cadence regular and slow. A gentle breeze stirs the trees, the ice-covered limbs tinkling like tiny bells. There is the crack of a not-so-distant bolt of lightning, and then, to her front, clearly through the mists of the melting snow, a line of Tibetan characters begins to coalesce out of the mist, the same letters seen on the *Korlo Gön-Poy* and the carving.

Drolma's eyes are still open, but with a new intensity as from the center of the circle, an object coalesces from seemingly nothing. It is spherical and transparent at first, perhaps as large as a full moon, and then, ever so gradually, tinted areas begin to appear— browns, greens, blues… patches of white. It is the earth.

The planet slowly rotates, serene in its universe, and then an object SLAMS into it with a brilliant burst of light!

Drolma cries out, *"Nya!"*, pitches forward and collapses into the total silence as the letters, and the planet, and everything else that was part of the visualization suddenly and silently vanish.

The silence is only then broken by the sound of a rising wind as it mournfully sighs through the trees.

WHITE HOUSE CONFERENCE ROOM

The President and the members of the National Security Council sit watching the large video screen on the wall to their front. The display shows almost the same image Drolma saw. An extremely accurate representation of the earth is shown rotating against the blackness of space, and then, almost too quickly to see, an object *slams* into it. There is a brilliant flash of light, and what looks like the results of a huge thermonuclear explosion begin to appear.

The President clicks the remote and turns the display off. He angrily tosses the remote onto the table. "Why do the bastards have to run this stuff on nationwide TV? What's the status of EarthShield?"

Secretary of Defense Lewis checks his notes as he speaks, "EarthShield 1 is scheduled for intercept in two weeks."

"What about number 4?"

"NASA says it's just a software glitch and they'll be back online within twenty-four hours."

"What about the French?"

Bradshaw jumps in, "They're standing by. They have the warhead and an Ariane launch vehicle ready to go at Kourou. All they need to do is fuel it up. And we've got a backup standing by at Vandenburg."

The President rubs his eyes. "Maybe we ought to black out the Hubble images from now on. Just in case."

Bennett shakes his head. "Wouldn't do any good. The asteroid's too close. All the major observatories can see it now."

The President shakes his head in resignation, "Great. That's just great."

Chapter 5

DECISIONS

LEH, LADAKH, OCTOBER 20

Ed, Angela, Jamie and Samten Rinpoche step out of a dusty four-wheel drive vehicle in front of a small inn. As they stretch and shake out the kinks, Ed keeps a protective hand on Jamie's shoulder. He looks around, then squints up into the bright midday sun. "Man, now that's a blue sky!"

Samten Rinpoche nods as he looks up. "We call it 'Tibetan blue', like lapis lazuli."

Two men exit from the inn and approach Rinpoche. The owner, Ponderji, holds his touching palms up in greeting, "I am Ponderji. Welcome to our inn."

Rinpoche returns the greeting and introduces the others. "This is Missus Angela, Mr. Ed, and Mr. Jamie."

Ed cuts in, "Just call me Ed. I'm not some damned talking horse."

Ponderji stares at Ed with some confusion—he can't imagine how anyone could mistake Ed for a horse. "I am happy to meet you all. Please, come inside. My man will take care of your baggage. Please come along."

As they follow Ponderji into the inn, Ed winks at Jamie. "I sure am hungry. Must be the air."

. . .

The next morning, Ed is sprawled out on his small bed, virtually exhausted and a little green behind the gills. There's a light tapping at the door, and he groans as he answers. "It's open."

Angela enters followed by Jamie and an attractive young Indian woman, who carries a tray and pulls an oxygen bottle on a small cart. Angela sits on the bed next to Ed. "How are you feeling?"

Ed rubs his raspy beard, "Like I was rode hard and put away wet."

Jamie, perhaps just a bit too brightly for the situation explains, "You've got altitude sickness—we're 11,500 feet above sea level."

Ed looks at him through painful eyes, "Why the hell are you so perky?"

"We were higher than this on the last trip. Anyway, it's harder on old people."

"Thanks so much for that info. And don't ever consider politics as a career." Ed finally notices the girl. "Who are you?"

The girl smiles sweetly, "I am Indira. I have soup and tea for you, and some oxygen to breathe. It'll make you feel much better." She places the tray down on a side table as Ed's eyes follow her every move—he's feeling better already.

"Huh. Think I will have some of that soup."

As Indira attaches a small nasal cannula to his face, Angela pats him on the hand. "Good. Rinpoche, Jamie and I are going to visit with someone." She points to a hand bell on the table. "If you need anything, just ring the bell. We'll be back in a few days." She bends over and kisses Ed on the cheek. "Get some rest."

Jamie pats Ed on the shoulder. "You'll feel lots better tomorrow."

Ed nods, "Thanks, doc."

As Angela and Jamie exit the room, Indira brings Ed his soup.

Angela and Jamie start to walk down the hall, but they can still hear Ed.

"India. That's a pretty name."

Indira laughs, "My name is in-DEAR-ah."

"Well, that's even prettier. You got a boyfriend?"

Angela raises her eyes in silent resignation as Jamie just grins.

MOUNTAIN FOREST—OCTOBER 22

A local guide slowly leads an exhausted line of hikers up a small hill.   Angela battles to stay up with him, but Samten Rinpoche has fallen behind.   Jamie walks along with Rinpoche, and the older man is struggling, fighting to catch his breath. "Woof! I spend too much time sitting!"

Jamie looks up the hill with concern, then smiles at Rinpoche, "Can't be too much more.   You can make it."

Up ahead, the guide and Angela approach a small stone hut. The burgundy robes of a lama are visible.

A few minutes later, everyone has arrived at the hut and they're greeted by Chökli Rinpoche. Samten Rinpoche smiles at his old friend as he speaks, "You constantly amaze me, Rinpoche. I am half your age but I cannot take another step."

"There's no need to. You have arrived."   He turns to Angela and Jamie, "It is good to see you again."

Angela nods as she speaks, "Nice to see you. We'll talk more when I can breathe."

The new arrivals all exhaustedly drop to the ground, just in time to see that their guide has already turned around and is walking back down the hill.

Angela points to the departing figure, "Where's he going?"

Chökli Rinpoche shrugs, "Home to his wife. His services are no longer required."

Jamie watches the disappearing figure, "How are we going to find our way back?"

Angela tries to laugh, "Easy. It's downhill all the way." She looks around. "Where's your friend?"

Chökli Rinpoche replies, "She will be here soon." He gestures to Samten Rinpoche to continue.

Samten Rinpoche turns to Jamie. "Jamie you must first understand why we are here. The *gau* you have been entrusted with contains a most sacred *pel-doong*. It is required in order to perform the *chö-ga-chak-lin*."

"Huh?"

"A kind of ceremony. It must be performed very soon. Drolma is the only person left in this world who can show us what is required. But, she must first meet with you to insure that it is possible."

Just the barest beginnings of suspicion are starting to form in Angela's mind. "What kind of a ritual is this?"

Samten Rinpoche shrugs. "Only Drolma knows."

At that moment, Drolma steps from out of the trees and walks toward the group. She wears her white tunic and pants, the same as when she stopped the hunter. She walks with the grace of her leopard, not boldly or aggressively, just very much *here*. The effect is charismatic.

Angela tries hard not to stare in fascination... *my God... she is a warrior woman... a shaman?...*

Jamie is all eyes. He turns to Angela and silently mouths, "It's her." Angela barely nods in agreement.

Both Rinpoches quickly stand. Samten Rinpoche is the first to speak as he presses his palms together in greeting. *"It is such a blessing to see you once again!"*

Drolma replies, palms pressed, bowing, *"It is I who is blessed, Rinpoche. It has been far too long."*

Chökli Rinpoche gestures toward Angela and Jamie. "Drolma, this is Angela Edwards."

Angela brings her hands up in greeting. *"Tashi delek."*

"Tashi delek," Drolma replies. "Do you speak Tibetan?"

"Very little, I'm afraid. Your English is excellent. It sounds American."

"I was taught by Americans." She turns to Jamie. "And you are Jamie."

Jamie, in spite of his shock at seeing this woman, brings his hands up in greeting. *"Tashi delek.* That's about all I know."

Drolma smiles at the boy. "Well, it's a good beginning."

Jamie is transfixed as he stares at Drolma. "I've seen you before."

Drolma looks at Jamie with interest for a moment, almost as if she's evaluating the goods. "We will go now."

Angela puts her pack back on as Jamie reaches for his.

Drolma turns to Angela. "Please wait here. We won't be long."

"Where are you going?"

"Just for a walk. To get acquainted."

"Wait. I want to know what's happened to my son. He's covered with writing that look like tattoos."

Drolma freezes for just an instant, then she catches herself and turns to Jamie. "Can you open your jacket and shirt for me so that I might have a look?" Jamie unzips his jacket, and pulls up his shirts. His chest is covered with the mantras, and now, the beginnings of some imagery have become visible. Drolma's outward calmness at seeing this hides her inner astonishment. All of it appears exactly the same as those seen on her brother, Lama Sang-Nagk, and her mind begins to race... *this cannot be!... how does this happen so quickly?...*

Drolma nods and smiles reassuringly. "Yes, this is <u>very</u> good. It is the prayer of the protectors. They will protect you against all harm. So, please tuck your shirts in and let us go while we still have some light."

Angela holds her hand up, "Wait. Are they ever going to go away? Can you remove them?"

Drolma nods, "Please, do not worry. They will disappear on their own when they are no longer required. And really, we must leave now."

Angela looks at Samten Rinpoche. He barely nods. Drolma turns and begins to walk away, into the woods, toward the mountains. Chökli Rinpoche motions for Jamie to follow her.

Jamie looks at his mother, "Mom, it's okay."

She nods, thinking ... *dear God, please make it okay... this is all so terrifyingly weird I just want to scream...*

Jamie starts off after Drolma. He pauses at the edge of the woods, looks back at his mother, then turns and disappears from view.

. . .

It isn't long before Jamie has dropped a few yards behind Drolma as the woman continues her methodical, steady pace through the trees. He stops to catch his breath and glances around—just behind, two snow leopards are pacing him.

"Holy shit!"

Drolma glances back. "Better catch up."

Jamie moves smartly right up behind her, and then watches wide-eyed as the beautiful animals walk alongside them, one on the right, the other on the left.

The sun is almost behind the mountains when Drolma finally stops. Jamie is near exhaustion behind her. She shakes out a rolled up sheepskin and spreads it on the snow.

Drolma removes her heavy coat, sits, and brings her feet into the lotus position. The two snow leopards drop to the ground to one side of her and begin to groom themselves.

Jamie walks up and drops on the skin next to the woman. He looks at her, "It's going to be dark soon."

Drolma studies the boy, "Are you afraid of the dark?"

Jamie notices she's not wearing her coat. He picks up his plastic water bottle—it's frozen solid. "No. Aren't you cold?"

"No. Are you?"

Jamie's "I'm okay" lacks a little conviction.

Drolma settles herself on the sheepskin. "Do you know how to sit?"

Jamie nods. "My Dad, he taught me some before he left."

Jamie arranges himself into a lotus posture, "Like this, right?"

Drolma glances at him approvingly, saying, "So far, so good." She falls silent.

Jamie looks around at the now dark forest and the sleeping snow leopards.

"You want me to do the sitting and the breathing thing now?"

"Yes, if you think you can manage it." Drolma's voice is calm and gentle, "So, what we have to do requires that your mind be calm and clear. We are in the perfect place to achieve this. There's no one else around to distract us, and we are safe, we are well." She pauses and watches as Jamie seems to settle a bit. "Perhaps we can begin to empty our minds... thoughts will come, that's natural, but just let them go... don't get involved with them... don't dance with your thoughts, just let them float on by... allow your mind to be calm... uninvolved... just observe... just sit... breathe... relax... just be..."

. . .

Some time later, Jamie and Drolma silently sit in the moonlight. She begins to speak, "I met your father some time ago."

Jamie cocks his head toward her, "Really?"

"Yes."

Jamie looks off into the trees. "He got killed climbing a mountain over here."

. . .

High in the Himalayan Mountains, two heavily clothed figures struggle through the night and the snow to a high camp on the mountainside.

Jake Edwards strains under the weight of an injured companion. His breath comes in gasps as he plunges through the snow. He turns his head to the person he is carrying, his voice straining over his labored breathing, "We're almost there!"

. . .

Jamie continues, "Some people got hurt and he went to help."

. . .

A figure appears out of the dark and calls out, "Jake-la!" The man, a Tibetan, takes Jake's injured companion. Then he notices that Jake is turning around to go back, just as a heavy snow begins to fall.

"Jake, where are you going? Camp is this way!"

"Got to get the others or they'll die out here!"

"It's too dangerous!"

"I can't just leave them!" Through the now heavy snowstorm, Jake turns and disappears into the night.

. . .

Jamie continues, "A really bad storm came up and he never came back."

The two sit in silence for a long moment. Drolma nods as she speaks, "Your father... he was a good and brave man."

"Yeah. I miss him a lot. So does Mom."

"And so do many others."

. . .

Chökli Rinpoche, Samten Rinpoche and Angela rest in the flickering light of a few butter lamps. There is no real furniture except for a pair of crudely constructed low tables and the piled rugs and sheepskins on which they sit. A metal teapot steams in a bed of red coals. A cup is next to each of them as they sit watching the small flames flicker.

Chökli Rinpoche breaks the silence; "I met your husband some time ago."

There is a long pause before Angela responds, "He was a wonderful man. He died climbing a mountain over here."

. . .

Drolma gently asks, "Why did your father teach you how to sit?"

Jamie shrugs, "He said it would help me to see the world the way it really is. He said that sometimes we go crazy and see stuff that's not really there. That sometimes our heads just make stuff up and that we believe it 'cause we kind of want to, even if it's dumb. He said it would be great if I could find some time every day, but especially when things got really weird for me. Then it would help a lot."

"And has it?"

"Has it what?"

"Been helpful."

Jamie squirms a bit at all of this questioning. "I don't know. Sometimes when things get intense I can do the breathing and that keeps me from going crazy."

Drolma is silent for a long moment as she continues to look at Jamie. "Actually, Jamie… he didn't teach you this just to help you. It's also to help others. In fact, it's mostly to help others."

The boy shakes his head, "Geez, helping others is the biggest thing in the world for all of you guys."

The slightest bit of an ironic smiles crosses Drolma's face. "Well, at least you've been listening. Let's continue. Place your hands on your knees. Now, sit up. Relax… imagine you are like a mountain. You are strong, you have substance, you sit grounded on the earth. You are calmly alert, aware of all that's around you. Like a mountain, imagine that your head is above the clouds. These clouds, they are like your thoughts and the cares of this world. They have no effect on the mountain and your thoughts and cares can not disturb you unless you allow them to. So, now… head straight, eyes gently focused on that stone to your front… just rest your eyes on it. And Jamie, there's always a space, a gap between the end of one thought and the beginning of another. Try to rest in that space."

. . .

Angela continues to stare into the fire. "Jamie misses him so much. So do I."

Samten Rinpoche stirs, "All who were fortunate enough to have known him remember his many selfless acts."

Angela is motionless as she speaks, "I just don't understand why he had to die so soon."

Samten Rinpoche sighs, "And neither do I."

. . .

Only the moonlight illuminates Drolma and Jamie. She turns to Jamie. "Remove your coat and shirt."

"Are you kidding? I'll freeze!"

"No, you won't."

Jamie looks at the woman for a moment, then removes his jacket, shirt, and strips down to the skin. His body is virtually covered with lines of the Tibetan characters. In the center of his back and on his chest, the characters form a circle. Drolma looks at him with wonder.

Jamie looks down at his chest, "Are they ever going to go away?"

"Yes, in time. Open the *gau* my brother gave you."

Jamie's hands go to the metal box. "He was your brother?"

"Yes. Lama Sang-Nagk was my older brother."

Jamie removes the *gau* and opens it.

"Remove the *pel-doong*."

Jamie does as he's asked. Drolma cups her own hands, saying, "Hold it in your hands, like this." Jamie looks at Drolma's hands. They appear strong and sturdy, yet seemingly undamaged by the harsh life she lives. He centers the relic within his own cupped hands.

"Jamie, this world is in terrible danger. There are billions and billions of beings whose lives depend on what we do. We must try to save them, but we must also truly want to save them. It cannot be only because we're afraid for ourselves—that won't work because there is a huge difference in intention, and intention is absolutely the most important thing here, and in life. Do you understand what I mean by intention?"

"Like, why we do something?"

"Yes. What we do must be for others, not for ourselves. What we will do is for them, not for us. Honestly, this is not so easy to accomplish. Many truly dedicated people spend their entire lives trying to... maybe you would say 'reprogram' themselves. We know that the strongest desire in a human is to survive. It takes a special person to place the survival of others ahead of themselves and the ones they love. Yes, mothers of all kinds will die for their children, we've all heard of that. But there are those people who willingly choose to sacrifice themselves to save another or others whom they have never met. That is extraordinary. And when they do, the most amazing things become possible. It's almost as if the universe chooses those moments to allow profound and positive change."

Drolma pauses and stares deeply into Jamie's eyes. "So, let's begin. Think of your father. See him. Remember how much you love him. Remember how much he loved and cared for you. Open your heart, allow your heart to fill with the warmth of this love. Really feel it, as if he were sitting here with you right now, right here in this place. Let that warmth of your love spread throughout your body, and provide you with comfort for you and everyone." She pauses for a moment as Jamie quietly stares ahead. "Allow yourself to truly feel his presence and this blazing love."

Jamie closes his eyes.

Drolma continues. "Can you feel it?"

Jamie takes a deep breath and sighs as a few tears begin to appear.

"Now, include your mother. See her next to your father. Let this feeling of love grow to include them both."

Jamie begins to slowly sway from side to side. "And my grandfather? Can he be there too?"

Drolma smiles, "Of course he can. And anyone else you care to include."

They sit for a while, and then Drolma continues.

"Jamie, this world is filled with so many beings, and all of them want only to be happy. The problem is most don't know what it is that will bring them true happiness. It will take time for them to learn how to achieve the happiness they seek. They could use a little help, Jamie. If you can find the love, you could include them all in your heart right now... even those who have proven difficult for you—"

"There's this guy at school who's always giving me crap. Every time I'm around him I get in trouble. Why would I want to make him happy?"

"Because he is in pain. Because he is suffering. Because you are really the same as him. Believe me when I say this; there is no difference between him, and you... and me. In fact, it is said that we all have been each other before, perhaps many times. "

"Is this that reincarnation thing again?"

"Yes."

"You really believe in it?"

"I do."

"Okay."

"<u>Everyone</u>, including those who suffer, those who have no one else who cares, those in despair, you can help them now. Really, as we sit here. Really, because we are all the same. The differences that you see are only because we are each in different circumstances. In our purest form, we are all the same." Drolma pauses for a long moment, then begins again, "All of this love that you have is in your heart. It is good that you have so much. But there's too much love to just stay there, it needs to flow out to everyone and everything. Look into your heart, imagine that it is overflowing with so much love, that this warm, caring love begins to spread around you, healing everyone and everything it touches, for as far as the eyes can see, for as far as the mind can imagine."

Jamie settles back into his sitting. The swaying begins again and as Drolma looks down at the boy's hands, the *pel-doong* begins to glow.

A moment passes and Jamie's hands themselves become luminous. And then, all of the characters on his body begin to softly glow as if lit from within.

Her voice is very soft, "When you open your eyes, gently look straight ahead."

Jamie's eyes slowly open. It only takes a few moments, but once again, the surrounding snow has begun to melt. Jamie's forehead is beaded with perspiration. His eyes blink and he tries to wipe his face with his shoulder. His hands are still glowing as he stares in wonder.

"Be still, Jamie. Be still, and see."

The mists are visible and again, the letters form, bending into a circle, and the circle begins to turn. Within its center, a huge three-dimensional image of the earth, just as clear as any NASA photograph, coalesces and begins to slowly rotate.

Jamie's eyes are almost popping out of his sockets as he watches this image continue its slow rotation... *this is so cool... it's like I'm in orbit*—he's startled by the sound of rolling thunder, the *crash* and *hiss* of lightning striking, as a brilliant streak of light flashes into the "atmosphere" of this earth.

A huge, blinding explosion instantly erupts on its surface and the image shifts from a single view of the totality of the planet to a series of images, almost like a timeline. They are cataclysmic, biblical in proportion, and accompanied by the terrible sounds of destruction and the wailings of tormented beings.

Devastating winds rip trees up by their roots and demolish cities, towns, buildings and homes. Huge forest and city fires burn out of control. Gigantic tidal waves sweep over the coastlines, destroying everything in their path. Volcanoes erupt. Enormous earthquakes split the ground, topple structures and cause huge avalanches.

Fearsome showers of lightning crash down from the twisting, violently colored skies. The skies then turn dark, and acid rain begins to fall. The rain turns to snow, and the few remaining figures on the surface struggle to find food, water, shelter. The snow stops, and the world is very dark and very cold.

When the skies finally clear, nothing but destruction is to be seen. Not a living thing is visible on the surface. To the naked eye, the world is dead.

The entire visualization suddenly compresses down into a brightly glowing red ball the size of a marble. Drolma holds her hand up, palm out, and the ball zips into it. She clutches it in her fist and her hand glows an incandescent white for a moment. Then the light fades away, and she places her hand back on her knee.

Jamie looks with astonishment at her. "How did you do that?"

She slightly tilts her head to one side, "What you should be asking is how did _we_ do that?"

Jamie looks at the calmly dozing snow leopards—none of what he has just seen seems to have registered with them. And then it comes to him.

"The rockets... they aren't going to work, are they?"

"There is something we can do, Jamie, but it will be very difficult. It will also be very dangerous. I cannot make you do it, I will not force you to try. But perhaps you can spend some time thinking about whether or not it is of interest to you."

"What is it?"

"It's a ritual, a ceremony, but, as I said, it's very difficult. And dangerous."

"What do you mean 'dangerous'?"

Drolma pauses... _how do I tell him?..._ "It is possible that you could die."

"Die? Like, dead? Like my Dad?"

"It is a possibility. If you decide that you want to help, you must ask yourself _why_ do you want to help, _why_ would you put yourself in such danger? It is also equally important that the decision is yours alone. In any event, I will not allow you to do this thing if I think you do not truly understand."

"Is it like maybe a fifty percent chance?"

"At this point, I don't know. Put your shirt and jacket back on before you get cold."

"Huh? Oh, yeah... right." He glances down at the characters on his chest. "They're still here."

"Yes, it is not yet time for them to be gone."

Jamie glances over at one of the snow leopards for a long moment. "Drolma?"

"Yes?"

"I could die?"

"It is a possibility."

"Why me? Why's this happening to me?"

"Because you... are you. You are *Dampa Garma Pawo*..." she pauses and smiles " ... and no one is more surprised than I!"

SPACE

In the darkness of space, the four EarthShield spacecraft fly in a line toward their moment of destiny. They are now individually strung out many thousands of miles apart, with the antenna-studded #4 bringing up the rear.

NASA MISSION CONTROL, HOUSTON

The EarthShield flight crew monitors the status of the spacecraft at their various consoles. The big screen down front now shows a split image: half is a real-time image taken from the camera on EarthShield 4, the other, marked TOP SECRET from a classified reconnaissance satellite. Both halves of the screen are dark except for the sprinkling of stars.

Suddenly, there is an *intensely bright flash* that quickly fades away. Then another... and finally, one more.

A General officer sitting at his desk looks up, "What the hell was that?"

One of the console operators yells, "Holy shit! They just detonated!"

The General looks at the screen in confusion. "What did you say?"

"All three devices just detonated! The whole freaking thing just blew up... sir!"

WHITE HOUSE, PRESS ROOM

It's pandemonium in the press room. Reporters and television cameras fill the space, jockeying for position. Suddenly the room falls silent as the Press Secretary enters and walks to the podium. He adjusts the mike, opens a notebook and begins to speak.

"Ladies and gentlemen. At nine o'clock this morning, Washington time, a group of terrorists commandeered a NASA communications facility in Hawaii. They were able to use that facility to transmit the firing codes for the EarthShield spacecraft. All three of the devices detonated."

The room explodes with voices. A reporter asks, "Were they captured?"

"They surrendered after transmitting the codes."

"Did they say why they did it?"

The Press Secretary pauses for a moment before continuing. "They said they believe that man has no right to interfere with God's plan for the cleansing of the earth."

A second reporter speaks out as he glances at his Blackberry, "I've just been told that one of those guys was Dr. Tim Gordon. He works for NASA and has ties to the Brother Leroy militia. Can you confirm that?"

"No comment."

Yet another reporter jumps in, "Does this mean the asteroid's going to hit us? Do we have a backup?"

The Press Secretary nods. "Of course. The French government is preparing to launch the backup to EarthShield. This was always an option and the launch vehicle and thermonuclear device were prepositioned for just such an eventuality."

A sea of reporters' hands waves for attention.

"Please, that's all for now. We'll have more this afternoon. Thank you." The Press Secretary turns and quickly exits the room.

SPACE

The huge, mountainous body now known as JAMIE'S ROCK silently hurtles through the blackness of space, toward the pale blue dot in its airless sky, a dot that is now much larger than before.

MOUNTAIN FOREST

Angela awakens to the low drone of the two Rinpoches chanting their morning prayers and the *click-click* of the beads of their *malas*. She looks around the small room for Jamie, then quietly slips outside.

She shivers, rubbing her arms as she tries to warm herself in the cold... *God, it's freezing... I hope Jamie's inside with a fire...* Angela begins to gather firewood, panting out clouds of breath condensation as she goes... *no one would ever believe how this has all turned out...*

Angela doesn't even see Jamie as he steps out of the forest, alone. He walks up almost behind Angela, still lost in her thoughts.

"Hi Mom."

Startled, Angela spins around, "Oh! Honey, are you okay?" They hug.

"Yeah, I'm okay."

She can see that he's on his last legs. "God, you must be exhausted. Where's Drolma?"

Jamie <u>is</u> exhausted, but his eyes are bright from an adrenaline high. He looks over his shoulder into the woods—there's no one there. "I don't know. She was just with me."

Chökli Rinpoche and Samten Rinpoche step outside. Jamie turns to them. "We're supposed to go back to the hotel, then come back here in five days. She'll be ready then."

"Ready for what?" Angela asks.

Jamie responds as if it should be obvious. "The ritual."

. . .

Inside the hotel kitchen, Ed is wiping grease from his hands as a young man picks up some simple tools from the floor. An ancient refrigerator, the cover to its mechanicals removed, is humming away. Ponderji stands beaming with satisfaction, shaking his head in disbelief, while Indira leans over a table preparing a meal. Her eyes rest lovingly on Ed as he speaks. "That thing will probably run another fifty years"… and then he mutters under his breath, "… if we've got another 50 years…"

Angela and Jamie walk in, dusty and tired from their trip. Angela smiles seeing Ed up and about, "I guess you're feeling better."

Ed laughs, "Hey guys. I've even got a job."

Ponderji is ecstatic, "Mr. Ed..." (Ed immediately winces) "... is a genius! He has fixed my icebox. He is a <u>very</u> good mechanic!"

Ed glances up, winks at Indira, adding, "I also got their TV working. Oh yeah, you probably haven't heard."

"Heard what?" Angela asks. Ed continues to wipe his hands. "The news. They just announced it. The 'EarthShield' rockets. Some religious wackos got ahold of the firing codes and blew them up."

Jamie freezes in place as Ed continues, "They're getting ready to launch a French rocket with another thermonuclear device on it, but it's going to be close."

Ed's words echo in Jamie's mind... *she knew... how did she know?... how could she know?...*

Ed looks at him—Jamie has a thousand yard stare in his eyes. "Jamie, you okay?"

The boy snaps out of it. "Huh? Yeah." He nods. "Yeah, I'm okay. I think maybe I'm going to take a nap... really tired."

Ed notices the markings on Jamie's arms—they're even darker than before. "He's still got those marks. Now what happens?"

"We go back," Angela explains. "In three days."

NOVEMBER 1

Several days later, it's a repeat of the last trip. A guide leads Samten Rinpoche, Angela, and Jamie, along with Ed up to the stone hut.

As they approach, the guide gives out a call, and Drolma and Chökli Rinpoche step out. They bring their hands up in greeting. Drolma smiles as she speaks, *"Tashi delek."*

"Tashi delek," replies Samten Rinpoche, a bit breathlessly. Angela and Jamie just bring their hands up. They are too winded to speak. Samten Rinpoche turns to Ed, "This is Ed, the father of our friend Jake."

Drolma looks at Ed and their eyes meet for a long moment. She nods, "It is good to meet you."

Ed smiles, but his eyes are carefully measuring Drolma as he speaks, "Likewise."

Drolma turns to Angela and Jamie. "A little tea will bring the spirit back into you. Come inside." She holds the door open for them.

Samten Rinpoche and Chökli Rinpoche settle down on the sheepskins, while Angela and Jamie almost collapse to the floor. Ed squats against the wall, seemingly right at home. Drolma hands each one of them a cup, then begins to pour the tea.

After a few sips, Angela and Jamie appear to have recovered their energy. Angela looks up at Drolma, pointing to her tea, "This is really something. What's it made from?"

Drolma is almost dismissive, "Just some herbs from the mountains. They only grow here." She pauses for a moment, then adds, "We will have to leave soon."

Angela looks up, "Leave? For where?"

"The ritual site."

"Okay. Just a few minutes and we'll be all set."

"Only the boy is required."

Angela, uncertainty registering on her face, pauses for a moment, "How long does this ritual take?"

"A few hours."

"So we might be able to get back tonight?"

"Sorry?"

"Jamie, Ed and I."

Drolma gently laughs. "Oh, no. We will have to travel to the appropriate place. It is a journey of at least twenty-one days, probably closer to a month."

The impact of Drolma's words hits Angela in her gut. "Where is this place?"

"Tibet."

"Tibet? Twenty-one... that's forty-two days round trip... that's... what?... six weeks? Or two months?"

"At least."

Ed has been watching this back and forth and now looks up at Drolma, "You've got to be kidding."

Angela angrily turns to Samten Rinpoche, "You knew this?"

"I did not, but I am not surprised. There are some rituals that can only be practiced in the appropriate location."

Angela turns back to Drolma, "You're going to sneak into Tibet and disappear for maybe two months?

Drolma shrugs, "There is no other way."

Ed sighs as he stands, "In case you've forgotten, the Chinese Army's all over the border passes."

The wind suddenly seems to go out of Angela, "This is crazy. The world is coming to an end, and now this wild woman wants to drag my son, who's been disfigured by God-knows-what, off into a hostile country because she needs him to conjure up a spell that's going to stop a billion ton asteroid from smashing into the earth. Ed's right. You people have got to be kidding."

Ed's had enough, "Come on, let's get the hell out of here."

Chökli Rinpoche turns his full gaze to Angela and Ed. "I can only imagine how strange and frightening this appears to you. I, too, am fearful of the task ahead, but, believe what you will, I am telling you with all the certainty that I possess, this world will absolutely cease to exist if the ritual is not done. Everyone and everything that you know and love, billions upon billions of beings, everything of beauty in this world, all of its history and knowledge... all will be destroyed and all will die. There is no other way. The recent setbacks have made that clear."

The Rinpoche's words stop all conversation for a moment. There are tears in Angela's eyes, "I can't lose my son, too."

The room is silent, and then Jamie speaks, "If we don't try, we'll lose everybody." He pauses, "I have to do this, Mom."

Tears run down Angela's cheeks as she looks at her son. "You're so much like your father."

"Mom, come with us."

Angela looks at Jamie for a long moment, then fixes Drolma in her gaze... *what have you done to us?*...

The woman regards Angela with unblinking eyes, then turns her gaze to Ed. "It will be very difficult."

Angela shakes her head as she speaks, "I can't believe this is happening. What if we just go back to the hotel?"

Drolma turns to Angela. "Truthfully, I do not know if you can do this. To even try, you need to truly believe that every one of us, every being on this earth is incredibly important. Yes, there is so much suffering, so many individuals doing terrible things. They are selfish like undisciplined children and they have even perverted their own spiritual teachings. But it is not hopeless. They need the time to learn, to make it right, but that time is running out. Every one of us has the potential to achieve something absolutely magnificent. Think of it—we could consciously become the most incredible of beings, perhaps the most wonderful in the universe. Beings of amazing wisdom and compassion! Think of the good we could do! But, if this world is destroyed now, then all of those potentials go with it. They will not return for a long time... an enormously long and dark time."

She pauses for a moment, closes her eyes, then continues. "That is why we most do everything we can to save them. I did not create this event. It was foretold one thousand years ago, and yet here we are now, together in this place because we each have a role to play. Even Jake Edwards had his role—were it not for him, we would not even be here now. And, please remember, with your own eyes, you saw Lama Sang-Ngak after he had surely passed from this world. He spoke to you. You must now realize that there is much more to this than you can yet possibly understand."

No one says a word. Ed looks hard at Drolma, "Let's say we tried to do this thing. Can you really get us where we need to go without being captured by the Chinese or freezing to death on some mountain pass?"

Drolma nods once, "Yes."

Ed continues, "Must be the altitude because personally, I think we've all gone nuts. I'll tell you one thing for sure though. You're not taking Jamie anywhere unless I go with him. And that's not negotiable."

Jamie reaches out and takes Angela's hand. "And Mom has to come with us."

Drolma looks at Jamie, Angela and Ed for a long moment. She nods, then reaches into a corner and pulls out what look like rags, but are homemade poncho-like jackets, hats, and mitten-like gloves. She hands them to the others. "Put these over your own clothing. They will keep you warm and help to hide you."

Jamie slides into his. Angela stands, unable to move. "Need some help, Mom?"

Ed shakes his head in resignation as he puts his on, "Every freaking one of us is certifiably nuts." He turns to Drolma, "I guess we don't need any more supplies, you've probably got that all figured out. Okay, I'll be tailgunner."

Drolma looks questioningly, "Tailgunner?"

"I'll bring up the rear... the last in line."

Angela pauses for a moment, then slides into her jacket. Chökli Rinpoche nods approvingly, then begins a low chant. Samten Rinpoche joins in. Over the low drone of the chant, Drolma acknowledges the blessing with a bow, and opens the door. Angela, Jamie and Ed slip into their packs, and step out of the hut into the afternoon light.

Drolma immediately heads toward the forest and the others hurry to catch up as the two Rinpoches step outside, still chanting.

Just at the edge of the forest, Angela turns and looks back towards the hut. She sees Chökli Rinpoche and Samten Rinpoche wave. Angela tentatively raises her hand, waves, then turns and disappears into the forest.

. . .

Much later, Drolma leads Angela, Jamie and Ed up a ridgeline and onto a small plateau. She pauses until they catch up, then walks over to a stone-covered depression in the ground. She reaches inside, pulls out a huge, homemade rucksack, and slings it onto her back.

Angela looks up into the sky, "It's getting dark."

Drolma turns to the others, "Yes. From here on, we should make as little sound as possible." Drolma turns and starts to walk again.

Jamie looks toward her, "Aren't we going to take a break?" Drolma continues to walk in silence.

"Doesn't look like it," Angela replies.

Ed nods knowingly. "This could be interesting," as they start off after Drolma.

Chapter 6

TRIALS

NEAR THE BORDER

Several nights later, the small party continues to walk through the bitterly cold darkness. There have been very few signs of human life in this rugged landscape—just the occasional footpath, maybe a blackened few rocks where someone once built a fire, and, of course, the inevitable strings of prayer flags that seem to say ... *yes, you are not the first to pass this way...* However, when Angela looks up toward a nearby mountain pass—faint lights are visible and the low *humming* sound of... a generator?... comes through the night. She catches up to Drolma and points at the lights.

Drolma puts her face close to Angela and Ed's, and whispers, "Chinese military outpost." Then she turns and begins to walk again.

. . .

It's morning, and now the mountainside is almost barren. Only a few small shrubs grow on the snow-covered ground. A pile of rocks is stacked against the mountainside to close off a fold in the ground.

Inside the "rock pile", a small space has been cleverly constructed, almost like an oddly shaped rock igloo with mud caulking to seal the cracks. As Angela and Jamie huddle together, exhaustedly sleeping in the gear they've brought, Drolma and Ed ease into the tiny space carrying a few pieces of dried dung and brush. They begin to arrange it for a fire.

A few minutes later, Angela opens her eyes. Jamie stirs to wakefulness as Angela sits up. It is incredibly cramped in this tiny place, yet there is a small, almost smokeless fire heating a teapot. Four cups and a bowl are laid out.

Ed whispers, "Just like home."

Jamie whispers back, "I'm still tired... and my head hurts."

Drolma looks at the boy and says, "We will eat, and then we must leave."

Jamie gazes into the bowl. "What is this stuff? *Tsampa?* Again?"

Drolma sticks her finger into the bowl and swirls it around. A kind of doughy paste forms around her finger and then she pops it into her mouth. "It's mostly barley, there's some butter, water and a few other things I sometimes add for variety."

Jamie sticks his finger into the bowl, but his swirling is not as productive as Drolma's. He licks his finger. "This stuff kinda tastes like dirt."

Angela dives into hers. "Eat it, you'll need the energy."

Ed fixes Jamie with a hard stare. "Better learn to love it. I got a bad feeling we're going to be eating a lot more of it."

Angela curiously glances at Drolma. "Don't you ever sleep?"

"Of course, but I don't require much," Drolma replies. She pours the tea and hands the cups to the others.

A few minutes pass and then Drolma emerges from within the rocks. She stays on her knees, moving slowly so as not to disturb anyone or anything that might be near. She carefully scans a full circle around, from the mountains down to a few feet distant, looking for anything that seems out of place. Then she motions for the others to come out. As they sort themselves out, Drolma puts her mouth near Jamie's ear, her breath warm on his cheek. "The mantra. When you breathe in, say the mantra. When you breathe out, say the mantra. Trust me, just doing this simple thing will keep you strong." She removes a *mala* from around her wrist and presses it into his hands. "You've seen me do this. Move your right thumb over a bead each time you chant your mantra. When you have done all of the beads and come back to the big one, flip it around like this," and her fingers expertly reverse the direction of the beads. "After ten times, slide one of the smaller counter beads down and start again. When we stop, show me how many you've done. Do you understand?"

"Yes."

They slip into their packs and start to walk. Drolma immediately moves with a fluid, steady gait while the others limp as they stretch out their cramped muscles.

. . .

The days and nights pass, marked by interminable walking and climbing. Drolma seems to float through the changing landscape, her breathing soft and deep and regular, her steps ever sure and precise. The others have struggled, but their aching bodies begin to adapt to the altitude and the terrain, the gasping becomes less intense, and the pure physicality of the exertion becomes its own moving mantra that allows the body to begin to pace itself as it learns how to move more gracefully, more efficiently through this beautiful but stark geography.

Then there are those magical moments when, perhaps on a flat plateau, after no one has spoken for several hours, the air warmed by a brilliant sun hanging in a "Tibetan blue" sky and stirred with just the most gentle of breezes, all of this enhanced by the sheer isolation and the quiet, the mind is allowed to lose itself as if expanding to take up all of the now available space in this magnificent environment, in long moments measured only by the endless footsteps that seem as if it would be just fine if they could go on forever.

Angela looks around and up into the sky... *no wonder they had so many masters... this place... it's magical... there really is nothing to do except let your mind... what's the word they use?... spacious... become spacious... the mind expands, becomes spacious... how could it not?...*

Angela's reverie is broken as the party approaches a jarring sight in this wild, seemingly uninhabited place—a rusted, weather-beaten sign. The metal post is held up by a large pile of rocks, its stark warning boldly scripted in Chinese, Tibetan, and, rather peculiarly, English:

"WARNING!
MILITARY SECURITY AREA!
DO NOT ENTER!"

As they walk by, Ed can't help himself as he takes another look behind and scans the hills to the left and right, looking for something, anything that might give a hint that they are not alone.

. . .

A furious, violent storm lashes the plateau, blasts of wind bend the rain so that it streams sideways in slashing horizontal sheets of water. Bolts of white-hot, purple and green lightning crash down on the peaks and valleys accompanied by the gigantic, almost deafening *crash-boom* of instant thunder.

From the shelter of a cave, huddled together near the entrance, Ed and Angela watch the storm, dumbfounded by its fury. Ed shakes his head in wonder, "I saw a tornado down south once but you know what? This has got it beat."

Angela is mesmerized by the storm. "God, I wish I had my camera now." She glances over her shoulder to look further back inside the cave where Drolma and

Jamie sit in meditation. "Never seen Jamie sit that still for so long." She turns back to watch the storm outside.

Drolma and Jamie sit next to each other, each with their legs in lotus, left hand on the left knee, right hand in front of their hearts, thumbs endlessly and rapidly pulling the beads of their *malas*, one after another. The violent sounds of the storm are muted here as they sit, eyes half-closed, the sound of their gentle breathing accompanied by the soft clicking of the beads.

Jamie softly inhales, and feels a brushing against his right arm. He glances over and sees Drolma's bent knee halfway up his arm. He turns back to resume his gaze to the front, then stops... *what?*... He looks back, and sees it... she is no longer anchored to the floor of the cave. Tilting his head down and to the side, he stares at the empty space beneath her floating form... *oh, man!*... As he turns his head forward again, her voice is very soft, so calm as she whispers... "... close your eyes... gently breathe... let go... allow yourself to rise up..."

. . .

It's near dark, and Drolma kneels between two large boulders on the side of the almost barren mountain. Her breath swirls in clouds of grey fog as she carefully searches the ground. She picks up a stone, positions it in her hand with some care, then smashes its pointed side into a patch of ice between the rocks. Her reward is the sound of gurgling water bubbling up, and she begins to fill the containers she has brought along. As she caps the first one, she stops, a puzzled look on her face, and glances up. A man in a white robe sits on the rock, smiling.

"Dear sister... it is so good to see you again!"

Drolma drops back on her heels and silently stares. Tears begin to flow from her eyes as a breathless sob shakes her body. *"Sang-Nagk! Brother! Are you truly here or have I gone mad?"*

Sang-Nagk chuckles, *"I often think we're all a little mad..."* He picks up a small stone and playfully tosses it towards her. It makes a loud *thonk* as it hits one of the water bottles. *"... but see?... I am here. How may I help?"*

Her palms come together at her forehead as she bows her head, squeezes her eyes shut and fervently whispers, *"Thank you, Lord Buddha, thank you!"*

She looks up, *"Dear brother, I do not understand how this has come to be. It took over forty years before the signs began to manifest on you, yet they are almost fully completed on this boy in a few short months. And he is now beginning to display some accomplishments. He has had no training to speak of, knows nothing of our traditions. How can this be?"*

"*My sister, it can only be that he is the true Dampa Garma Pawo. I knew it the moment I saw him.*"

"*But what am I to do with him? He cannot possibly perform the ritual without destroying himself, and possibly the others. He has a fine heart and his intention will be as pure as possible for one so young and inexperienced but it's not the same as you or me. He does not have the kind of realization that you, or even such a poor example as I possess.*"

A faint smile crosses Sang-Nagk's lips as he speaks, "*You wonder why you weren't chosen, don't you?*"

Drolma's face clouds as she shakes her head. "*Not even for a moment. It is heresy for me to even think of such a thing.*"

Sang-Nagk continues, "*And yet, here you are, with what appears to be an imperfect choice, burdened with the task of somehow assuring that what absolutely must be done, is done.*"

"Yes, my brother. How am I to accomplish this?"

Sang-Nagk's form begins to shimmer as it becomes more and more translucent. His voice takes on a distant quality as he replies, *"This is as much your task as it is his. It is your transformation that is the key. Look into your heart, dear sister, that magnificent heart that you still deny."* And then he is gone.

Drolma silently sits for a very long moment, eyes still focused on the now empty place where Sang-Nagk appeared. Her arms reach out, aching to touch some remaining essence of his presence, then close in and wrap around herself as she embraces only the painful emptiness, as if the substance of her own body is to be its only companion this lifetime, and she gently rocks back and forth.

Her eyes drop to the ground to her water bottles and she sees the rock he tossed. She picks it up, wraps her hands around it and holds it to her forehead for a long moment with closed eyes, then slips it into an inside pocket of her jacket.

. . .

Jamie's eyes are nearly frozen shut as the snow continues to fall. He blindly feels the rope around his waist, hanging on for balance, the other end tied to Drolma, who is visible just a few yards to his front against the snowy incline. His breath comes in bitterly cold gasps that sting the nose, throat and sear the lungs as his legs burn from the exertion of each step... *got to sit down for a second... can't breathe... just rest a little...* he stumbles, tries to catch his balance and in doing so steps off toward the edge of the ridgeline... and is suddenly looking down at a valley, several thousand feet below.

The change in tension of the rope startles Drolma and she spins around. What she sees freezes her heart— Jamie is hanging between her and Angela, over an opening in the snowfield, an overhang having collapsed in his inadvertent misstep. He is suspended by the rope with nothing but thousands of feet of air between him and the valley floor below.

Angela drops to her back, holding on to the rope with all of her strength, digging her heels in, trying to keep Jamie from falling and to prevent herself from being dragged over to the collapsed overhang. Ed frantically digs his heels into the snow, pulling on the rope attached to Angela.

Drolma keeps tension on the rope as she moves away from the edge, back toward Angela, traversing a large half circle. Her added strength stops Angela and Ed from sliding any further toward the edge.

Jamie stares down into the abyss, his chest fighting against the tightening rope that makes it almost impossible to breathe as it bites into his skin, his mind fighting back the panic that begs for release through a throat-rasping scream of sheer terror. As he helplessly hangs in the air, he hears a faint voice... Drolma's... "... breathe, Jamie... breathe..."

Somewhere inside, something gives Jamie permission to let go... to relax... to breathe. The raucous cacophony of sound in his head slowly dies down and his body calms. And then, in wonder, he looks down on himself from above, amazed at how calm this boy is who looks just like him as he hangs in space, so far above the rocks below, with nothing nearby to even try to reach for a handhold, to even *begin* to think about using to climb up, and he thinks that really, he should just float up. Why not? And then he's back in his body, so calm, so peaceful as he thinks, ... up... just float up... *what did she say?... "... let go... allow yourself to rise up..."*

Drolma is the first to feel the tension in the rope begin to lessen. She turns to Angela and Ed, "Pull, very gently but steadily."

Jamie appears at the surface, then slightly above it as Drolma carefully steers him away from the edge. Ed and Angela stare in wonder, still hanging on to the rope. Drolma crosses over to the boy and gently presses him down to the snow. She brushes the snow from his face. "Jamie… look at me." The boy's eyes open. "Let it go… take a deep breath… good. Yes. Does anything hurt?"

Jamie tries to catch his breath. When he speaks, the words fall out between his panting for air. "I'm sorry. I tripped or something. I'm really tired. I'm sorry."

Angela wraps her arms around Jamie as Ed staggers over. He turns to Drolma, confusion in his eyes, not knowing whether to be astounded or just angry. There are icicles hanging off of his now longer beard. "He's exhausted and we damn near lost him and maybe the rest of us. We've got to find a place to hole up and rest."

Drolma turns and points up the ridge. "The top is right up there, then we go back down. We can't stay here, it's too exposed and too high but the place where we are going is just past and a little lower down. It will be much easier walking and safer to rest." She stands, checks the rope and helps Jamie to his feet. "So, you can go a little further, yes? Then we can rest."

Jamie nods and turns to Angela and Ed. "I'm okay." They sort themselves out and, once again with Drolma in the lead, begin to walk through the falling snow.

. . .

At a nomad's camp one night, several of the nomads,
along with Drolma and Ed are dancing around the fire to the
sounds of drums, a flute and a horn. They shuffle, stomp and
spin as Drolma leads Ed in ever more complex steps. She
takes Ed by the hand as they dance, and looks at him with a
smile of love, totally unerotic, but with absolute and radiant
purity, as if to say, "... I will take care of you..."

Ed awakens with a start—he looks around.
There's no camp, no nomads, they are all jammed inside
another rockpile shelter as a fierce storm blows and
shakes the ground. Angela and Jamie are huddled
together, sleeping fitfully.

In the light of a butter lamp, Drolma sits, quietly
chanting a mantra while thumbing the beads of her *mala*.
She glances at Ed, who has gotten himself back together
and now gazes at the flickering lamp. The beads never
stop in her fingers as she speaks. "You saw war as a
soldier?"

"Yes. A long time ago."

"How did you find it?"

"I thought we were the good guys. But all that
killing... pain... such a waste."

Drolma nods, "So, you've learned something
since then?"

"Maybe." He snorts in disgust. "Too bad it took so long."

"But you have learned. Some never do."

"Yeah, it's so obvious now. Why didn't I know then?"

Drolma shrugs, "You did what you thought was necessary. That is all one can ever do."

"Still, I should have known better."

"You will the next time."

The wind roars outside. Ed sits for a moment and then looks curiously at the woman, as if to ask... *next time? what next time?*... but she's back to counting the beads on her *mala*. He looks at Angela and Jamie. "They don't look so good."

Drolma nods, "Fatigue and the altitude. We will find a place to stay for a few days to allow their bodies to rest and acclimate. And how are you feeling?"

"I'm okay. Pretty much have a headache all the time."

Drolma points to the teapot. "Drink more of this tea. It will help. It will help all of you." She goes back to her beads.

. . .

Ed awakens again. The storm has subsided, but Drolma has gone... *now what?... how did she get out of here without waking everyone?... why am I even asking?... she's a ghost...* he drifts off back to sleep, and then blinks awake again.

Drolma's return is as silent as her departure... she just suddenly appears, silently sliding into the tiny enclosure and folding herself into her original place. She gently shakes Angela and Jamie. Their slow awakening and bleary eyes show their fatigue.

"We will leave now. There is a nomad encampment in the direction we must go. It is quite large and we don't have time to go all the way around it. So... we must be even more quiet than we have in the past, but we must still walk quickly. That means we must walk very carefully so as not to make any noise that will alert the people, the livestock, the horses or the dogs. We must be completely silent, like ghosts. Take a step, then carefully take another. Place your foot slowly on the ground. Make sure you are on the ground and not on a stone, a piece of wood, or worse, a hole. Then do it again, over and over. Silently. Don't kick a stone... don't stumble... don't open a pocket on your clothing... don't whisper... total silence is required. Again, be completely aware of each step, how your feet touch the earth. Don't look at any of the animals you might see... most will be asleep but they may sense your interest if you do. Do you understand?"

The others, their eyes a bit wide with concern, nod that they do.

"Good. Stay very close to me and to each other. It's time." She blows out the lamp and instantly, it is pitch black.

Drolma leads them out into a moonless night, with only the faint, ancient light of a billion stars tossed against the velvet blackness of the sky dimly illuminating their way as they begin walking toward the edge of the encampment, their breath creating momentary clouds of fog.

Drolma seems totally alert, yet moves with a relaxed, fluid, animal-like grace. Angela and Jamie are acutely focused on their own movement, while Ed walks more naturally, as if he's done this kind of thing before... and he has... *just like poopin' and snoopin' through the weeds... looking for the bad guys... smell 'em before they know you're there... never thought I'd do this again... I think I've missed it...* He carefully scans around, and to the rear... *good... nobody there...*

As they pass the tent-like structures, snoring and coughing can be heard. A baby cries. There are low, muted bits of conversations here and there.

Drolma suddenly stops as an untethered horse slowly walks toward her. Everyone freezes.

The horse stops right in front of her. He shakes his head, snorts a cloud of fog, and looks around. Drolma hasn't moved a muscle, nor have the others. The horse bends its long neck to the ground and snatches some grass, chews for a while, then moves off in another direction.

Drolma slowly begins to walk again, and the others follow.

. . .

Some time later, they are off the plain and moving through low hills. Drolma stops, turns to the others and whispers.

"Wait here. I won't be long," and she is gone. Ed silently moves up and sits with his back to Angela and Jamie, facing in the direction from which they have just come. The three of them are still, touching back-to-back, each looking in a different direction, silently watching, waiting. They sit, alone with empty minds in this empty place, exhaustedly calm, so far away from anything that they have ever known before. In a way, they could have just as easily been sitting on the moon, or each of them on a different moon in this total, still silence.

After a while, Drolma returns without a sound. They stand, and once again, begin walking, following Drolma's lead.

. . .

It is that time of the very early morning when the new day has not yet cast its light on the world, but everything is still... quiet... waiting. Drolma and her party approach a series of large rocks on the steep side of the hill. She stops, and motions for those behind to follow her lead as she drops to one knee.

After a few minutes, Angela questioningly touches Drolma on the arm. Drolma barely touches the woman's hand in response, but never turns her head— she is on alert, waiting, watching.

And there he is... a man? Who or whatever, stands not ten feet away from them, as if out for a morning stroll, face hidden inside the hood of a robe. In the dim starlight, weathered boots are barely visible as is a long walking staff in one hand, and the rosary with a crucifix around the neck. He or she turns around, and Drolma rises, motioning for the others to follow.

They silently walk for some time as they make their way into the rocky hills, around gigantic stone boulders, following no discernible path or trail. As they round one of these huge rocks, the robed figure steps into the darker shadows... and disappears.

Drolma follows, then Angela, and Jamie... but not Ed, who has paused for a moment to look behind at the strange, landscape to his rear, covered with roundish boulders of varying colors, almost like one would imagine to be found on another planet, becoming more and more visible as the very beginning of the dawn's light slowly pushes back the dark curtain of the night.

Ed turns to continue, and sees no one, nothing except for a gigantic rock to his front with a complex series of fissures and shadows. He looks around, then fights back a rising sense of panic... *damn!... just like a newbie... I lost visual contact...* He looks around again, then checks the ground for tracks. There are none except for exactly where he is standing... *what the hell...?* He takes a couple of steps, and watches with fascination as his previous footprints disappear... *okay Ed... deep breath... this is weird... they'll find you...*

Jamie steps out of the shadows, grabs Ed's hand and pulls him into the rock... and through it!... into a narrow tunnel.

"What were you doing, Grandpa?" he whispers.

"Checking to see if anyone was following us." Ed looks behind him, trying to see some kind of an entrance. There isn't one.

They make a few turns, and then enter a cavern. Light has already begun to stream down from somewhere above what passes for a ceiling.

The cavern is spacious, but not huge. There are a couple of small, handmade low tables holding books, scrolls, and a lantern. A simple stone altar with a cross is on one wall. There's a rough sleeping area, a small wooden frame with a mattress of woven thick cord on which blankets are piled. A few pots for water are next to a small charred area that once held a fire.

Jamie and Ed sit next to Angela. Drolma is seated next to the robed guide, who has removed his hood and reveals himself to be an Asian man of indeterminate age, but possessing eyes that reveal a deep kindliness with a sparkle of humor. She turns to the others and introduces him.

"This is Shénfù John. We will be staying with him for a few days while your bodies acclimate to the altitude, and to rest a bit." She turns back to Shénfù John and introduces the others in Chinese.

"This is Jamie… and Angela, his mother… and Ed, his grandfather, the father of Jake."

Shénfù John smiles and nods to each of them. His voice is soft, almost like the wind, with just the slightest trace of an accent.

"Please forgive my old voice... I don't often speak, but I am very happy to meet you."

Angela bows and says, "Thank you."

He returns her bow, "You are safe here and most welcome."

Jamie can't hold it back any longer. "The cross... are you a Christian? I didn't know there were Tibetan Christians."

Shénfù John turns to Drolma, "There were some in the early 1900s. Today, not so sure."

Drolma asks, "Did you know them?"

"A few, when I was passing through."

Ed perks up at this revelation. "Umm, you were there then?"

Shénfù John nods. "Short time."

Ed presses on. "Sorry, don't mean to be out of line here but wouldn't that make you well over one-hundred years old?"

Shénfù John laughs as he shrugs. "I'm old! But good health!"

Angela turns to Jamie, "Honey, I don't think Shénfù John is Tibetan."

Shénfù John's eyes sparkle as he turns back to Jamie. "I was born in Yinchuan, during the Qing." He pauses, "You are surprised I am Chinese?"

"I didn't think the Chinese liked the Tibetans. At least the ones I've met don't."

Drolma nods her understanding, "The truth is complicated, Jamie. We do have many Chinese friends. Some are Buddhist and respect our traditions and culture, some are simply kind and above politics. However, they cannot openly express that support. The government has taken a very hard line on anything that they think might lead to giving us any control over our lands and our lives."

"But you're different religions."

Shénfù John turns to Drolma, whispering in Chinese. She begins to translate into English, "We are more alike than you might think. Many Christians find wisdom in the teachings of the Buddha. Many Buddhists find wisdom in the teachings of Jesus. And if you want to learn about Love, you should also read Rumi. Yet, there is only one Truth, and our different cultures and histories have chosen to emphasize the differences rather than to celebrate the similarities."

The old man suddenly switches to a whispery English and looks intently at the three Westerners. "What I have found is that the further your separation in time from the One who introduced the original seekers to the Truth, the greater the likelihood that this 'current truth' has become that which was not originally presented. The original precious teachings became clouded, sometimes perverted, their original intent changed by unfortunate misinterpretations, unskilled translations, and deliberate changes to suit individual desires. That is why it is so important to seek knowledge from those who have kept their gifts as first presented. It is very, very difficult to find this now which is why we have so much discord in this world. The Hindus speak of a time of Kali Yuga, the Christians speak of the End Times. Both are descriptions of a descent into periods of spiritual darkness and of great hardship for all. Many agree that we have already entered this time. Others believe that we may be passing through toward its end. One can only hope the latter is true." He laughs, and gently shakes his head, "Too many politics!"

Jamie has been sitting, mesmerized by the old man's words. "Were you ever able to find the real Truth?"

Shénfù John's kind eyes peer into Jamie's. "More to the point, will you recognize it when it appears before you? Will you be perfectly open to the Truth when it is revealed? Or will your ego do you the distinct disservice of trying to 'protect' you from experiencing that which is already a part of you?"

Jamie sits in silence, as do Angela and Drolma.

Ed, who has been quietly sitting all through this, looks up, "Sorry, but I'm still trying to figure out the truth of how we got into this place. I didn't see an entrance, even when Jamie found me."

Shénfù John glances at Drolma, who fields the question.

"It's something one has to learn."

Ed looks at Shénfù John. "So you can do all of that magical kind of stuff?"

Shénfù John laughs again. "I'm a simple hermit monk. I spend my days and nights meditating on the love of God, praying that all of the beings on this world will find happiness. That is all." He sits for a moment in silence, then adds, "Now, you are safe here. Please, take rest." He has barely finished his words before Jamie, his head now hanging awkwardly forward, nearly pitches over in a profound sleep. Angela carefully slides the boy over to a pile of blankets, removes his backpack and pulls his sleeping bag out, draping it over the lightly snoring boy.

LHASA

Mr. Hsi, his thinning, dyed hair still slicked back, sits in his typical, government bureaucrat's office, smoking a cigarette that hangs from his lips as he makes notes on the stack of papers to his front. A television to one side shows a Chinese soap opera, the sound barely audible.

He glances out of the window toward Sun Island, surrounded by the Lhasa River, and stares at the hotel where he had lunch only an hour ago. The food was quite good and he was able to spend some time with one of his favorite lady friends in the suite the hotel keeps reserved for him several days a week. It was the bright spot in another dreary day in this strange place.

His concentration is interrupted by a knock on the door and a thin, young Major from the People's Liberation Army appears. Mr. Hsi looks up. *"What can I do for you, Major?"*

The Major walks up to the desk and places several photos in front of Mr. Hsi. *"General Zhang is very upset that these subversives have entered the Forbidden Zone. He asks if you have any reservations should it become necessary to eliminate them."*

Mr. Hsi picks up a magnifying glass and examines the photos. The enlarged images of the long distance surveillance photos cause him to sit in silence for a long moment, thinking... *now what in the hell are these people up to?... why are they with that crazy troublemaker? that man, maybe he's CIA... hell, maybe she's CIA...*

He looks up at the Major, "*Please inform General Zhang that one is a young boy. One is his mother. Two, maybe three are Americans. It is possible there could be political repercussions if they go missing.*"

The Major suspiciously stares as he looks at Mr. Hsi. "*You know these people?*"

"*They were here filming the barbarian ruins,*" Mr. Hsi replies. "*I have no idea what they are doing in this area. I certainly gave them no such authorization. Frankly, I can't imagine how they even got there, since they had an assigned driver and guide.*"

The Major picks up the photos, salutes, and leaves without another word. Mr. Hsi sits for a moment, lost in thought as he smokes, then goes back to his paper shuffling.

SHÉNFÙ JOHN'S

It is late afternoon in the cavern. Ed, Angela and Jamie are all sound asleep. Drolma and Shénfù John sit working their beads as they look at the three sleeping figures. Shénfù John barely moves as he speaks. *"They are totally exhausted and the boy is ill. I do not believe that just two days' rest is enough, especially if you must return."*

Drolma shrugs. *"It's all the time we have. We must arrive on Gönpoy-Ri very soon. Do you have anything else that might help them?"*

Shénfù John's eyes stay on the sleeping figures. *"I do have a more powerful herb. You'll take some with you but you must insure that they drink it every day. However, it can be dangerous to continue to use it after three weeks or so."* He pauses for a moment. *"This is an immense challenge that you face. You have done wonders with this child. His very special gifts are being quickly revealed because of your efforts. I would be so pleased to spend time with him at some future date. However, you know full well that for now, his abilities are so delicately balanced on a knife's edge. I don't envy your task, but I know that you will do all that you can. I will pray for your success."*

Drolma brings her hands to her heart. *"Thank you, my friend. Your blessing means so much."*

The two silently return to their practices.

. . .

It is night, and the small flame-lit lamps cast a dim light within the cavern. Drolma gently wakens Jamie, Angela and Ed. They stretch, scratch, and shake their heads, rubbing their eyes. Angela looks around. "I guess it wasn't a dream. How long have we been asleep?"

Drolma has gone back to a very small cooking fire and is preparing bowls of food. She doesn't look up as she speaks, "Almost two days."

Ed turns to her in amazement. "Two days? Feels like two hours."

Drolma brings the food to them. "Please, eat. We must leave soon."

Angela looks questioningly at Drolma. "How much further is it?"

"We are quite close. It won't be too long now."

Jamie glances over at Shénfù John, who is sitting in front of his alter, practicing in silence. "Is he going to eat?"

Drolma shakes her head. "I'm rather certain that he has had nothing but water for over twenty years now."

Ed looks over at the sitting monk, then turns back to Drolma. "How does that work? Does he run on batteries?"

"At this stage of his life, what you would call 'real food' becomes a hindrance to his further purification. What nourishment he requires comes from his practice."

Ed doesn't even blink as turns back to his bowl. "Right. Got it."

TIBETAN PLATEAU, DECEMBER 1

The late afternoon sun has already dipped below the high mountains and the air is still. The panorama of silent mountains and cloudless sky stretches for as far as the eye can see. Nothing seems to stir in this quiet tableau… well, almost nothing.

There is a bit of movement near a particular rock formation, as Drolma and Jamie slowly move their bodies in coordinated yoga sun salutations, reaching and stretching in unison as they deeply breathe and flow through the ancient *asanas*. After a while, Drolma drops to her knees. "There. That's better, yes?"

Jamie drops down beside her. "Yeah." He takes a drink from one of the several water bottles they've brought to fill at the almost invisible spring. He wipes his mouth and stares off into the distance. "Will it hurt a lot?"

"Will what hurt?"

"You said I could die. Will it hurt?"

The words slam into Drolma like a fist to her heart. She closes her eyes as she deeply breathes, taking a moment to collect herself before she speaks. "I never said that you would certainly die because of the ritual. I said there was a chance that it could happen."

"So? You never told me what the chances are."

Drolma turns to the boy, reaches out and adjusts his parka. "I don't know what the chances are. If I did, I would tell you. What I can tell you is that if it is necessary, I will give my own life to save yours. And frankly, I personally am in no hurry to leave this most interesting life any sooner than necessary. So, put away those morbid thoughts. And we should get back before the others begin to worry."

"Okay." Jamie begins to stuff the water bottles into his bag as Drolma picks a few more leaves from a low growing bush, stuffing them into her own sack. She looks up, and slowly begins to walk down the hill, *mala* in one hand and tears in her eyes as Jamie follows closely behind.

. . .

Under an intense sun, Drolma, Angela, Jamie and Ed continue their march across a barren and desolate high plateau.

They stop for a rest, and Jamie staggers from exhaustion. He looks at Drolma, "How much further?"

Ed retrieves a GPS receiver from his pocket. "According to this thing, we've been in Tibet for over a week."

Drolma takes Jamie's water bottle from his pack and hands it to him. "We're almost there. Drink."

Angela looks around, "You said there was a mountain. Where is it?"

Drolma points to her front as Angela stares over the woman's hand. She shakes her head in confusion, "I don't see it."

Drolma glances over her shoulder as she replies, "You will. We must go now."

Jamie looks up, "Really? We just got here."

Drolma points to the rear, "We are being followed."

Ed pulls a small pair of binoculars from his pack. He scans off into the distance, "Chinese soldiers, maybe eight or so." He brings the binoculars down. "Okay, Drolma. Now what?"

Drolma turns to the others, "Quickly, we must go. Stay close enough to touch me and each other!"

Drolma begins to quickly walk, and then she starts to just… *disappear*. Angela reaches back for Jamie's hand, then quickly grabs for Drolma's coat as Ed latches on to Jamie's jacket.

Almost instantly, their world transforms from a sun-blasted Tibetan plateau to a totally featureless, foggy landscape. Drolma continues to quickly walk through this fog as Angela hangs on to her coat with one hand as she uses the other to hold Jamie's. Ed tightens his grip on Jamie's coat.

The fog begins to thin and the surroundings take on an ominous appearance as Drolma slows her pace. It's a barren, raw world, the air warm and sulfurous. There are small earthquakes and deep rumblings. Lightning strikes nearby, punctuating Drolma's now continuous chanting.

. . .

The Chinese soldiers have arrived at the plateau. They warily look around as a helicopter circles overhead. There's no one there.

One soldier goes ahead, staring at the ground, *"Look! The footprints just stop… there's nothing more!"* He looks up into the sky as if he half expected to see them flying. He grabs the radio off of his harness and looks up at the helicopter, *"Eagle-two, can you see them?"*

The response crackles out of the radio, *"Nothing. Don't see anyone or anything."*

A second soldier spits on the ground, *"They are going to the devil's mountain! Shit on this! We should get the hell out of here!"*

The first soldier angrily looks around again, then barks into his radio, *"Eagle-two, pick us up. We're leaving this place!"*

. . .

Ed's eyes sweep around him. The landscape has begun to change again. Within only a few steps, the hellish environment is gone, replaced by fields of waving, green grass under an incredible "Tibetan blue" sky. It is warm, almost spring-like. Angela and Jamie are wide-eyed and begin to open their parkas. Drolma leads them to one edge of the field and slips out of her rucksack.

Ed reaches for his GPS again. He stares at the screen, "This is impossible. We're out in the open, there's not a hill in sight and there's no signal." He looks up questioningly at Drolma, then glances back from where they came—there are no soldiers to be seen. "Where'd they go?"

Drolma looks up from her rucksack, "We are in a place that exists next to the one where we normally exist. The entrance is available only to those who have been taught to see it. We need to be here to take the next step. To the soldiers, it appears that we have simply vanished."

Ed tries to get the words out, "How... I mean, is it... is it real?"

Drolma pauses for a moment as she speaks, "What is real? What is reality? Everything is defined by the quality and intensity of its many vibrational levels. Light, energy, the nature of all that we perceive, all of this can be understood in this way. Sang-Nagk knew how to 'see' in this way, and how to use this knowledge when required. He shared some of his knowledge with me. It is how the entrance to Shénfù John's home is manifested. I don't think it can be explained in words— it is something that must be consciously experienced. It is something that you need to 'see'."

She motions for the others to come close. "I need to make some adjustments. Jamie, come next to me." Drolma knots a cloth around Jamie's wrists and loops the boy's hands around her neck so that he's standing behind and against her back, his face over her shoulder.

Jamie tries to adjust his body as he stares at her. "What's this for?" Drolma doesn't answer as she squats, picks up her rucksack and puts it on backwards so that the bag hangs to her front.

Drolma turns her head toward Jamie, "Wrap your legs around my waist. I'm going to have to carry you for a bit." She wraps her arms around Angela and Ed's waists. "Hold hands across my back on top of Jamie, very tightly."

Angela and Ed shoot each other one of those *"now-what-are-we-doing?"* looks, and then link hands. Drolma's eyes close and an expression of deep concentration appears on her face as she begins to walk forward, moving Angela and Ed along with her. They walk for a few yards, and then... step off into an abyss.

Angela, Jamie and Ed are completely taken by surprise and their breath freezes within their lungs. Drolma's grip on them tightens as they plunge into the darkness. And then, the four of them, as if some strange four-headed creature from a dream, begin to, well, not fly, but they're not falling either.

Ed fights a sudden flash of vertigo as he glances down... then up... it's all the same... there's nothing to see... *what the hell is this?... are we moving?... my gut says we're not falling... I think we're moving but I don't feel any wind...*

They pass through an almost featureless darkness for a while, seeing only fleeting bits of shadow, until finally, a dim light returns and gains in intensity.

Moments later, a moonlit ledge becomes visible above them. They pass up and over it, and drop to the snowy ground with a *thump.*

They all sit in thoughtful silence for a long moment. As Drolma releases Jamie's wrists, Angela, a look of pure confusion on her face, just stares at the woman.

Drolma brushes off the snow. "We've passed through to where we need to be." She stands and motions for them to follow her. "We still have a way to go."

Chapter 7

RITUAL

THE SUMMIT OF *GÖNPOY-RI*, DECEMBER 7

Under the moonlit sky, the wind-swept mountaintop is deserted. There is no trace of Lama Wangpo's body. Only the broken remains of the prayer wheel's mountings and the bent oilcan are to be seen.

It is too windy to speak as Drolma points to the small cave entrance. They stumble towards it through the darkness.

Inside the cave, Drolma fills one of the butter lamps with oil that she retrieves from inside of her parka. She lights it and looks around—everything is still as it was, but now covered with a light dusting of blown-in snow.

Ed looks at his GPS again. "I give up. Where are we now?"

Drolma answers as she sets things straight in the space, "We are on *Gönpoy-Ri*, the Mountain of the Protectors."

Angela shakes her head. "This mountain... there was no mountain."

Drolma continues to set things in order. "This mountain exists in this world, but not as you would normally see it. Take rest while I make tea."

. . .

The space has been cleared of snow, the small cooking fire is lit and all are sitting, quietly drinking their tea. Drolma begins to speak.

"Almost a thousand years ago, the father of our lineage, Jikmé-Pawo, was a powerful leader and a devoted follower of the Buddha's teachings."

. . .

Jikmé-Pawo, a physically powerful and well-dressed man grows weary of watching his two friends try to move a rock that has fallen across a mountain path, blocking their way. He moves them aside, laughing as he says, "Please, allow me because if you don't, we will surely spend the night here!"

His two companions step aside as he puts his shoulder to the rock, and, with a magnificent display of effort and a loud "Ho!", manages to roll the rock off the edge of the path. Dusting his hands, he steps to the edge and peers over. He freezes, his face horror-stricken.

His companions rush over in alarm as Jikmé-Pawo suddenly turns and runs back down the mountain. Their faces register the terrible thing they see and they, too, rush after him.

Jikmé-Pawo rounds a turn and finally arrives at what has caused him so much anguish—a man lies dead, crushed by the rock Jikmé-Pawo has dislodged.

Several days later, a terribly distraught Jikmé-Pawo meets with one of the greatest enlightened masters of that time, Tokden-Ö-Zel Rinpoche, at the monastery in which he resides. With tears in his eyes, he tells his story.

"Because of my carelessness, because of my haste, because of my inattention, and worst of all, because of my pride, I have done this terrible thing. What can I do to atone for this?"

Tokden-Ö-Zel Rinpoche pauses for a moment before he speaks. "Only two months ago, this good and decent man, the one whose life you so unfortunately ended, had come to me with a very disturbing vision. He had seen a future world destroyed in a fiery death to all but the lowliest of beings. He, too, asked what he could do. I gave him a prayer and instruction to help prevent such a catastrophe. He promised to dedicate his life to this purpose."

He pauses for a moment, then continues. "Now, he is gone—his work is undone. Perhaps you can help. Is this of interest to you?"

. . .

Drolma continues her story. "Tokden-Ö-Zel Rinpoche took Jikmé-Pawo as his student and empowered him with the necessary knowledge and skills. For almost a thousand years, a few chosen descendants of Jikmé-Pawo's lineage have continued his task. They have kept the *Korlo Gön-Poy* constantly turning, here on this mountaintop, that its prayer may never cease. Now, an infinity of karmic streams have converged, the *Korlo Gön-Poy* has stopped, and the destruction of this world is certain."

Drolma nods to Jamie. "You may open the *gau*."

Jamie pops it open and Drolma reverentially offers the palm of her hand as she directs their attention to the *gau*'s contents.

"That is the prayer given to Jikmé-Pawo by Tokden-Ö-Zel Rinpoche. And that piece of bone is from the skull of the kindly old man who only wanted to help save this world."

Jamie stares at the *pel-doong* with a look of awe as Angela shakes her head.

"Why Jamie?"

Drolma continues, "My brother knew that some day, the one who would finish this work, the one known as *Dampa Garma Pawo*, the one who would save this world, would appear." She looks at Jamie. "You are that one. You are *Dampa Garma Pawo*."

She reaches into her jacket, removes a small bundle and carefully unwraps it. It is a picture of Jake. Ed, Angela and Jamie's eyes lock on the photo as Drolma continues.

"A number of years ago, here in Tibet, there was a time of even more harsh repression. Lama Chökli and I were part of a group who wanted only to preserve our culture, our way of life. We came to organize a peaceful demonstration against the invaders."

She pauses for a moment, lost in thought, and then turns to Jamie.

"Your father, Jake Edwards, learned of this, and asked if he could come with us to take videos, to document the demonstration. We explained that it would be dangerous, especially since he was a foreigner. He said that the story was too important and the rest of the world needed to know what was happening. No one could talk him out of it—he insisted. So, he came with us. When the demonstrations began, the invaders quickly sent in the army, and then they began to shoot us. Many, many people died. And I did the worst thing that I, an ordained nun, could ever do."

. . .

The central square of Lhasa is awash with protesters trying to flee the gunfire of the Chinese soldiers. One soldier has cornered a dozen monks and nuns. He raises his AK-47 to fire.

. . .

Drolma's eyes close for a moment as she continues. "I could not let that soldier kill those gentle people. I could also not let that soldier take on such terrible karma for himself."

. . .

Drolma throws herself at the soldier, wrestling his weapon from his hands as they both fall to the ground, and then BLAM! The rifle fires into the chest of the soldier.

. . .

Drolma's eyes are downcast as she speaks. "This soldier, just a boy, really. I took his life, hoping to save others. And, as one of the prime organizers, I am also responsible for the loss of all the others."

A long pause... "We were hunted like animals. I was injured." She looks at each of them individually as she continues. "Your father, your husband, your son, arranged for our escape. It was my life that he saved the night that he died."

Angela, Jamie and Ed are stunned.

"It was he who carried me to Lama Chökli, then turned around to go back for another. I have prayed for him and for his fortunate rebirth every day since."

Ed obviously wants a closer look at the photograph. Drolma hands it to him, and he looks at it for a long moment. He flips it over, and, on the other side, is a photograph of Jikme. He stares at it for a long moment, as he unconsciously strokes his beard.

"Jake Edwards saved my life. Sang-Nagk found you, Jamie, and you discovered the asteroid. So many things have happened. You see, we are all a part of this. Our karmas are intertwined in ways we cannot begin to comprehend. But really, all that's important is that you are the one, this is the time, and we are here, at the place."

No one says a word for a long moment, and then Drolma looks up. "We have so much to do."

CHEYENNE MOUNTAIN OPERATIONS CENTER, DECEMBER 7

The President sits with Dr. Johansson, Secretary of Defense Lewis and several of his advisors as they watch the Battle Staff at their state-of-the-art communications and display stations.

"How long before the detonation?"

Lewis points to a countdown timer, "About fifty minutes."

The President turns to Dr. Johansson. "What about the debris?"

Dr. Johansson shakes his head. "If we get hit by ten or twenty half-mile diameter pieces, we're not much better off."

The President continues to stare at the countdown timer. "What's the earliest we could get hit?"

"That won't change—December 31st."

SHERMAN OAKS, CALIFORNIA

On a residential street in Sherman Oaks, California, a northwestern San Fernando Valley suburb of Los Angeles, a family finishes loading their SUV as if they are going on an extended camping trip. A man in his mid-forties emerges from the vehicle and calls out toward the house.

"Come on, guys!"

His wife brings one last sack of groceries to the vehicle as their teen-aged daughter talks to her best friend off to one side.

"See ya."

Her friend nods. "Yeah... maybe... I hope so. My folks are staying here. They say there's nowhere safe to go."

"My Dad thinks we can hide up in Big Bear. I don't think it's going to make any difference. How can you hide from a freakin' asteroid?"

The father calls out, "Sweetie, we need to leave now!"

The daughter turns and walks toward the now idling SUV. She looks back over her shoulder, gives her friend a sad wave, and gets inside the vehicle. It immediately pulls out into the deserted street and roars off.

GÖNPOY-RI, DECEMBER 9

Inside the cave on *Gönpoy-Ri*, Angela, Ed and Jamie watch transfixed as Drolma carefully assembles the replacement wheel, a complex marvel of beautifully polished and carved wood, whose many parts interlock together with a solid precision that requires no fasteners or glue, a piece of construction that would bring a smile to the face of a master machinist. She carefully slides the last piece in, checks the assembly one last time, and then lays it down on the small shrine. She looks up.

"We are almost ready. Do you remember the words?"

Angela and Jamie reply, "Yes," in unison.

Ed nods, "I think so. I'll follow along."

Drolma stands and picks up the new *Korlo Gön-Poy*. "It will take me a few minutes to prepare. Please be ready when I call." She disappears through the entrance.

On the wind-swept summit in the early morning dawn, Drolma works with infinite care and precision. After affixing the new *Korlo Gön-Poy* and its mount, she removes a thick red cord from around her neck and uses it to secure the fins on the top of the wheel as she folds them flat against the wheel itself.

Drolma picks up the oilcan and *klick-klocks* the plunger, filling the reservoir in the mounting shaft. She steps back, examines the *Korlo Gön-Poy*, and gives it a perfunctory spin. It's perfect. She replaces the oilcan, carefully examines everything again, then raises her eyes to the sky. Her gaze seems to see all the way to the end of the universe as her breathing slows; her eyes close, and her palms meet in front of her heart as her *mala* swings from her wrist. She turns toward the cave and shouts into the wind,

"Dampa Garma Pawo!"

Angela and Ed step out, followed by Jamie. He wears only the *gau* around his neck, a piece of white cloth that looks almost like a short sarong, and is barefoot as he walks through the snow. In the early morning light, the characters on his body are now much more prominent, the lines alternating in colors of red, yellow, green, blue and white.

He opens the *gau* and carefully removes the *pel-doong*, cupping it in his hand as Drolma begins to chant in an amazingly deep, rich voice that resonates with complex, pulsating overtones, a vibrating sound that seems to shake the air,

"Om Jeek-Ten Dee Kyohb Hoong...
Om Jeek-Ten Dee Kyohb Hoong..."

Over and over and over again, the pace of her chanting quickly increases until the words flow in an unending stream and the separate syllables are impossible to discern, almost as if it has become a river of never-ending song.

The *pel-doong* in Jamie's hand begins to glow with a deep red color, and then increases in brightness as it becomes whiter and whiter. The boy's hands begin to glow themselves, mimicking that of the changing *pel-doong*.

Angela and Ed have stopped in their previously assigned places and watch with a concerned, fearful fascination as Jamie's entire body now begins to glow as if lighted from within, further accentuating the multicolored Tibetan characters covering his body. His appearance is otherworldly.

Angela stares at Jamie, her eyes widen with what... love?... as she whispers almost to herself, "My God, he's so beautiful!"

Jamie moves next to the *Korlo Gön-Poy* and carefully slides the *pel-doong* into a space designed for it in its central mast. He steps back and begins to chant, and it's shocking—his voice is incredibly deep, resonant, almost painfully loud, filled with overtones that one would assume would be impossible for a human, much less this boy, to produce.

"Om Jeek-Ten Dee Kyohb Hoong…
Om Jeek-Ten Dee Kyohb Hoong…"

Just like Drolma's, his chanting becomes incredibly rapid until it, too, sounds as an uninterrupted river of music.

The *Korlo Gön-Poy* begins to glow with the same, otherworldly luminosity as Jamie, first more reddish, then increasing in brightness to a near white as Jamie chants… and then it begins to fade back to a near red.

Jamie continues to chant, but the expression on his face shows confusion and bewilderment as his voice begins to crack back and forth between the booming and powerful flow and that of a young boy. He struggles to maintain his strength, but now his knees begin to buckle as if he's being pressed down by an immense force.

Angela's fist is at her mouth as she and Ed watch in horror, neither knowing exactly what to do.

Drolma shouts above it all, "Angela! Ed! Chant with us! Give it your heart, he needs our strength!"

Angela looks at Jamie, the words frozen in her throat, and she runs over to him, not knowing what to do, except to stand behind him and wrap her arms around her son, and try to hold him up, to protect him, to do something… anything. She, too, staggers under the impact of the unseen weight pressing down on him.

Ed glances at Drolma, then runs over to help Angela, wrapping his arms around both her and Jamie. Like them, he begins to sag under whatever it is that is pressing them all down.

Drolma dashes over to Jamie and pulls Ed back, then Angela, shouting, "You cannot touch him now! Get back! It will kill you!" She flings them both back away from Jamie with such force that they fall on their backs onto the snow. She stands behind the boy, and pauses for a moment, looking up into the sky, and softly says in Tibetan, *"Please forgive me, but I have to at least try."*

Tears stream down Drolma's face as she wraps her arms around the boy. Her chanting increases in volume,

"Om Jeek-Ten Dee Kyohb Hoong…
Om Jeek-Ten Dee Kyohb Hoong…"

Instantly, there is a silent explosion of light that persists in its brightest intensity. Both Drolma and Jamie are enveloped in this unbelievable brilliance, so intense that it seems as if they have both become translucent.

Ed and Angela are knocked down on their backs again by this blinding light, shielding their eyes as they try to watch.

There is an instant, seemingly impossible increase in the intensity of this blinding white light—one would be forgiven for thinking you could actually *hear* it, as if the light had a physical force, and could surely be seen hundreds if not thousands of miles away.

> *"Om Jeek-Ten Dee Kyohb Hoong...*
> *Om Jeek-Ten Dee Kyohb Hoong..."*

The sound of the chanting rocks the very ground and the air seems to shake. Jamie and Drolma are visibly and violently vibrating together, so much so that there are moments where the two of them seem superimposed on stationary copies of themselves, looking almost like glass sculptures that appear for a flash, then jerk to a different angle of view. But then, there's an instant when one can see that it's not a vibration... in reality, they are rapidly flashing in and out of this existence.

Suddenly, the restraining cord on the top of the *Korlo Gön-Poy* SNAPS, the fins spring out, catch the wind and the *Korlo Gön-Poy* begins to turn, then rapidly spin.

Drolma's body instantly jerks up in an uncontrollable rictus, her eyes roll up in their sockets, and she collapses, falling backwards onto the snow where she remains motionless.

Jamie continues to stand, and the wheel begins to whirl faster and faster. A few tiny bits of light fly from Jamie to the *Korlo Gön-Poy*. Then more and more, until a cascading torrent of what look for all the world like sparks or fireflies flows toward the wheel from Jamie, who is now simply a blindingly white, vibrating, flashing figure. Suddenly, it becomes apparent that it is the Tibetan characters that are streaming from Jamie's body. Thousands and thousands of them flow into the *Korlo Gön-Poy* as it pulses brighter and brighter.

The *Korlo Gön-Poy* begins to fling these brightly glowing characters out and away from it, completely enveloping everyone and everything on the summit, as if they were in a sea surrounded by tiny glowing creatures. More and more of the brightly glowing characters fly off the rapidly spinning *Korlo Gön-Poy*, forming a giant, whirling, thundering, inverted vortex that screams upwardly, spinning into the sky... an upside down tornado of millions of bits of light that becomes ever larger and moves ever higher.

SPACE

As the gigantic asteroid hurtles through the blackness of space toward the earth, something very subtle begins. The entire asteroid is gradually surrounded by tiny sparkles of light, as if it had just been enveloped by a billion fireflies. These sparkles begin to fall into the surface, and everywhere they touch, the tiniest of fractures appear.

The surface of the asteroid is instantly crazed with a million fractures. Puffs of gas appear out of the cracks and quickly disappear into the vacuum of space.

More and more of these cracks begin to form, and Asteroid 2014 BD looks as if it's expanding in size. The space between the cracks continues to grow, and in just a few moments, the asteroid is no longer one giant piece of solid rock. It has been transformed into a swarm of small rocks that are slowly beginning to split themselves and to drift away from each other.

CHEYENNE MOUNTAIN

Inside the Cheyenne Mountain command center, an Air Force general speaks into his headset.

"Ten minutes to detonation."

All eyes are focused on the giant wall display screens. An officer at one of the stations taps the keys on his display as he speaks into his headset, "Stand by! I'm bringing EarthShield 4 up!"

One of the large displays flickers, and then the image of the asteroid appears. Another officer looks in amazement. "What the hell? It's getting bigger!"

The first officer stares at the screen. "I don't—no, wait… it's like… is it breaking up?"

Dr. Johansson stands and stares at the display. "My God, it is! It's breaking apart!"

The President puts down his telephone and looks up. "What's happening?"

Dr. Johansson can barely tear his eyes from what he's seeing. "It could be heating up as it gets closer to the sun. Maybe there were large deposits of frozen gases inside that are expanding. Maybe the damned thing was mostly ice all along. I just don't know. Now we've got to track all those pieces—"

The General cuts in. "Doctor, the French see it too. They say to detonate the device now or it'll be out of range."

The President looks at Dr. Johansson, the question in his eyes.

"I'm... I'm not sure... I mean, this changes everything!" Dr. Johansson looks helplessly at the President.

The President glances back up at the display and calmly says, "Fire it."

Dr. Johansson's turns to the President, "We don't know—!"

The President cuts him off, "We only get one shot." He looks at the General. "Do it!"

The General keys his headset, "Detonate the device!"

Several seconds pass, and then there is a *huge, bright flash* from the screen on the wall... and then the image goes dark.

The General looks at the President, "Detonation confirmed and EarthShield 4 just got cooked. We're going to track with radar now. It'll take about thirty minutes for things to settle down before we begin to know what we've got."

The President nods. "Then we wait. I hate waiting."

Chapter 8

WAITING

GÖNPOY-RI

Lama Sang-Nagk walks up from the cut in the rocks to the summit. He pauses, carefully examining the scene as he looks around.

All traces of the *Korlo Gön-Poy* are gone—the supporting mount, the wheel itself, the box for the oil can... all of it is gone. There is not a splinter of wood, not a sliver of metal, not a drop of oil to be seen.

The four figures lying on the snow are motionless. Lama Sang-Nagk begins to quietly chant as he kneels next to Ed. With great care, he places his hands on either side of Ed's face, brings his own forehead down and touches it to Ed's as he blows puffs of air toward the man's lips. A small vial of oil appears in his hand and he carefully places a single drop on Ed's forehead, between his eyes. He then reaches into his robe, removing a small bag. He takes a tiny round brown ball from the bag and places it inside Ed's mouth.

He crosses over to Angela and does exactly the same things.

He moves over to Jamie. The boy lies on his back, his young body now free of any markings, save for what might appear to be a number of small bruises. The *gau* is still around his neck, and he thinks... *so much has happened since we first met... and you have done so well...* Lama Sang-Nagk repeats the same actions he performed on both Ed and Angela. He sits up, then gently strokes the boy's hair and places his palms on Jamie's head, slowly sliding them down his neck, shoulders, arms and then his torso and the rest of his body until he reaches his feet. He repeats this several times until he has touched every part of the boy's body, chanting all the while.

Finally, he crosses over to Drolma. He smiles... *dear sister... is this the peace you so longed for?...* He performs the same ministrations to Drolma that he did to Jamie.

Later that evening, with the sky already darkening and the stars beginning to appear, Lama Sang-Nagk sits on the snow, with Ed, Angela, Jamie and Drolma lying to his front, arranged like a fan. Each is dressed in their normal clothing, propped up with their packs and rucksacks on their backs, and all appear to be in a deep sleep. Lama Sang-Nagk sits, absolutely silent and still for a few moments, and then, in an instant, they are all gone, vanished, without having left a trace.

SOMEWHERE...

"Sister."

The voice enters Drolma's consciousness as the lightest of whispers, a delicate, infinitely soft, feather-like touch... the tiniest hint required to cross the threshold to awareness.

She is pulled back from... *what?... an indefinable emptiness?... no, not emptiness... omniscience?... that's a little grandiose—*

And with the beginning of thought, Drolma's eyes open, and she deeply breathes. She looks around and sees that she appears to be on the top of a mountain, on a small plateau, but there's nothing to be seen around it. One could easily assume that it just appears to be in the middle of a world composed of... light? The sky is blue, the sun seems to be warm but isn't visible anywhere, the air is still... and Lama Sang-Nagk is to her front.

...how is that possible?... I was just looking that way and I didn't see him...

Lama Sang-Nagk sits, looking at Drolma with soft eyes.

"So."

The word enters her consciousness, but, curiously, his lips haven't moved. She begins to speak, but finds it hopelessly clumsy to even attempt. Instead, it's so much easier to just look at him and "speak" in her mind. *"Jamie… the others… where are they?"*

"They are… waiting."

"Where?" There's no response. *"Where are we?"* She looks around, *"I do not recognize this place."* Lama Sang-Nagk is silent. *"Am I in the bardos?"*

Lama Sang-Nagk glances around. *"Well, we're always in one bardo or another."* They sit in the stillness for a few moments.

Drolma looks up. *"I… I don't remember anything after I touched Jamie."*

"How does all of this feel to you now?" asks Lama Sang Nagk.

"Quiet… empty… and uneasy. I don't remember if it is done. Brother, were we successful? Is it done?"

"You accomplished all that was required. Do you understand that? Whatever success has been attained, it is because of your efforts… you have done very well, indeed! The final outcome has yet to be determined. Except for the return trip, your efforts are complete.

What happens next is not our concern." Lama Sang-Nagk sits for a moment before continuing. *"As for the others, they will remember an arduous travel and a fascinating ceremony. The rest, as far as they are concerned, will be a bit confused. They may think it's because of the effects of fatigue and altitude. Jamie, in particular, simply has no way of comprehending what happened after he placed the pel-doong. For him, for a while, it will be as if he went into a fitful sleep, marked by strange dreams."*

Drolma nods, then asks, *"And what of his accomplishments? He is already developing siddhis."*

"And as you well know, they require constant practice and attention. If he is so inclined, then the issue will resolve itself. I am more concerned about what becomes of you, dear sister. What will you do now?"

Drolma stares off into the distance for some time. *"I'm not sure."*

"The best way to preserve our gift is to live it, and to teach. Might that be something you would consider?"

She smiles, almost laughing, *"Who would want such a strange creature as me for a teacher?"*

"I can think of one who might very well <u>need</u> you as a teacher."

Drolma curiously looks at her brother. He settles into a relaxed posture as his next words enter Drolma's mind, *"When the time comes, you will know. Now... please... sit with me."*

They both sit, in silence, gazing at the expansive view that surrounds them... and then they are gone.

TIBET

... the Nothing is replaced with the flash of a four-pointed golden star that quickly fades back to not quite nothingness... and the beginnings of an audible awareness of the wind...

Jamie opens his eyes. He looks up into the sky, and, with no thought required, he simply takes in what he sees.

It is dusk. The sun has already passed below the mountain peaks, and the soft, fading light reveals the side of a tall mountain, pockmarked with shadowy entrances to small caves.

Just outside of one of those caves, within a sheltering rock formation, Drolma sits, looking toward the fading light in the west. Jamie glances to his left—his mother appears to be asleep next to her gear. To his right, Ed lies in a similar state.

A sound finally makes its way into Jamie's consciousness. It is Drolma's voice, so soft and gentle, whispery and lilting, singing a simple song. She gently sways in time with the words, her fingers tapping the rhythm on her knees.

One by one, the others begin to stir, stretching their limbs, looking around, a little dazed, a little disoriented. Angela looks for Jamie, sees him and touches his hand. "Jamie, honey, are you okay?"

"I'm okay, Mom." Drolma has come down to them and sits on a rock. Jamie turns toward her, "Did it work?"

Drolma smiles as she speaks, "You did all that needed to be done. And you did it very well."

Ed has been following this and looks around, "We're not on *Gönpoy-Ri*, are we?"

"No," Drolma replies. "We're some distance away."

He shakes his head. "How did we get here? I don't remember leaving or anything after all of that incredible light—"

"They're gone!" Everyone turns to look at Jamie, who now has his shirt halfway up as he stares at his chest. "The mantras..." his voice tinged with disappointment, "...they're all gone."

Chapter 9

NEW YEAR'S EVE

TIBET-INDIA BORDER, DECEMBER 31

It is late at night as Drolma, Jamie, Angela and Ed sit outside of another tiny rock pile shelter. The night is calm, the sky crystal clear, as Drolma quietly whispers her mantras and works her beads. Ed looks at the screen of his GPS and tries to figure out why the tracking history for the two weeks they were near *Gönpoy-Ri* is missing… *it's like we just disappeared and then reappeared…* He sighs, shuts it down, then stares off into the sky and waits with the others.

Jamie and Angela sit quietly talking.

"Are you scared, Mom?"

Angela smiles, "A little."

Jamie nods, "Me too." He reaches for Ed and clasps his hand. "I'm glad we're all together."

Angela and Ed each drape an arm around Jamie as they look up into the sky. Ed squints as he looks, "You know something? There are more stars here than in L.A."

Jamie laughs, "That's 'cause there's no light pollution… uh oh…"

Drolma raises her eyes as Jamie points up. Hundreds and hundreds of bright flashes streak across the sky. Angela kisses Jamie on the cheek. "I love you, honey."

"I love you too, Mom. I love you Grandpa."

Ed wraps his arms around them, "Back atcha' guys. Hang on!"

Drolma gazes up as one particularly bright streak travels across the sky, it's flaming tip narrowing as it disappears behind the mountains toward the north. She finds her lips silently forming its destination… *"Lhasa…"*

FARGO, NORTH DAKOTA

A small concrete building sits in the middle of a wind-swept snowfield, surrounded by security fences topped with razor wire.

Inside the anti-missile tactical operations center, officers and men of various services man battle stations as they track the incoming debris. An officer at a console stares at his display and speaks into his headset in a clipped, rapid-fire burst of words. "I've got over one-thousand incoming at mach... Jesus, it says mach eighty-two!"

A second console operator reports, "Roger that. I confirm!"

The General Officer Battle Commander keys his mike as he stares at his own display. "Priority alpha! Fire at will!"

The fields outside of the tactical operations center suddenly erupt in flame and smoke as volley after volley of high-speed interceptor missiles rocket into the sky.

. . .

In another snow-covered field outside of Moscow, a similar installation lies half-buried into the side of a mountain.

Inside the Russian operations center, it's pandemonium. The Russian General Battle Commander yells into his headset, *"Fire! Fire everything!"*

. . .

Above the earth, the thousands and thousands of rocks that are the debris from 2014 BD begin to glow from red to white-hot as they slam into the atmosphere. Just below them, several hundred missiles scream upwards and there is a moment when the outer atmosphere of the earth is filled with hundreds and hundreds of explosions. Many of the rocks are turned into dust, but, there are far too many for the missiles to engage and hundreds, perhaps thousands of separate pieces of 2014 BD make it through the explosions, the friction of the Earth's atmosphere, and plunge down, down, down toward the earth's surface in fiery trails of light, down toward the waiting billions below.

. . .

In an Andean mountain range, a sudden and loud impact triggers avalanches of snow and rock on the valley below.

. . .

In rural Idaho, an incandescently bright spear of light slams directly into the Brother LeRoy compound.

. . .

In mid-Atlantic, several streaks smash into the surface of the ocean creating huge waves. A nearby ship is drenched with the falling water, then wildly rocks back and forth but survives.

. . .

In a French country village, the patrons of a bar in the middle of their New Year's Eve celebration are knocked off of their stools by the shock of an impact. They pick themselves up, dust themselves off and immediately demand another round.

Chapter 10

AFTERMATH

LHASA

Military fire and rescue vehicles crowd the street. Smoking rubble in a crater is all that remains of the building housing the Tibetan Autonomous Region, Mr. Hsi's offices, and the local military headquarters.

Mr. Hsi arrives in his car and climbs out. He stares at the destruction, then looks around. Nothing else is burning, and it appears to be the only strike in the entire city. A Chinese military officer runs up and salutes.

"Was this a barbarian terrorist attack?" Mr. Hsi snaps.

The officer looks puzzled for a moment before he replies, "*No, sir. It was a piece of that asteroid. We think everyone was gone from the building when it hit.*"

Mr. Hsi looks up into the sky with a sense of unease. His eyes then go to the neck of the officer—beneath his uniform shirt, a red cord is barely visible around his throat. Mr. Hsi reaches for the cord and pulls it out—attached is a small jade pendant of a Buddhist deity.

The officer is near panic as he speaks, "*It… it was a gift from my – !*"

Mr. Hsi cuts the officer off with a wave, turns and walks toward the building. He pauses, and stands staring as the fire brigade sprays water, his eyes drawn into the hypnotic flames, and he sees…

… beribboned horses, their armed riders carrying multicolored banners, prance past huge crowds of Tibetans waving white katag offering scarves. The sound of crashing cymbals, drums, and horns fills the street as monks in elaborate costumes jump and spin in the air —

"*Did you know that Lhasa means the 'place of the gods' in our language?*"

An old Tibetan woman dressed in the traditional attire of *Kham* stares at Mr. Hsi.

"*What? No. I did not.*"

She turns back to view the flames with him as they both watch in silence. Then she looks up into the sky, *"They are not pleased at how this has all turned out. One wonders what new surprises they may have."*

Mr. Hsi stares at the woman, then silently turns and walks back to his car.

WASHINGTON, D.C., THE WHITE HOUSE

The Presidential Emergency Operations Center is fully staffed, plus everyone else who could squeeze in. All eyes are on the large displays on the wall showing various areas in the world that have been struck by asteroid fragments.

Secretary Lewis sits next to the President and Dr. Johansson, pointing to the displays.

"Incredible. No major population centers destroyed although you're not going to believe this one—remember Brother LeRoy, the leader of that fringe sect that stole the firing codes?"

"How could I forget?" replies the President, rolling his eyes. "Aren't they all in jail?"

"Most are still in custody, but their compound took a direct hit. I mean, a real hit. Must have been more than a few impacts close together."

"Any casualties?"

"We don't know yet. A team is on the way to check it out. There are a few forest fires here in the US and Russia. Minor hits in Europe, pretty good one in the Peruvian mountains. Small strike in the capital of Tibet. Most impacts were in uninhabited areas; hundreds of small hits in the oceans. Not one really big impact anywhere. Two pea-sized hits on the International

Space Station, but no injuries and no breaching of the hull."

The President shakes his head in wonder.   "Did the Russians shoot any down?"

"We confirm 480 for us, 75 for the Russians. "Thousands got through, though.   There were just too many and they were too fast."

The President turns to Dr. Johansson.   "Guess we're going to have to do a better job of looking for these things."

Dr. Johansson nods.   "We'll need lots more funding."

"I'm going to boldly predict that even this Congress won't give me much grief on that," the President observes.

A BORDER VILLAGE, INDIA

It's little more than a wide spot in the road. Drolma, Angela, Jamie, and Ed sit waiting under a tin roof shelter. Jamie's shorts and t-shirt reveal that his skin is indeed clear—the markings truly are gone. He looks at Drolma.

"Did we really save the world?"

Drolma smiles. "It was saved. That is all that matters. You cared enough, you *all* cared enough to go through so much to at least try." She looks off into the distance down the road at the old car that is kicking up a rooster tail of dust. "So, I think it's time for you to go."

Angela looks up. "You're not coming?"

Drolma shakes her head. "No."

Looking down, Ed kind of kicks the dirt, "So, where *are* you going?"

"I will return to Ladakh."

"To do what?" Angela asks.

"To sit for a while. To consider what has happened, and how I may best serve in the future."

Ed sticks his hand out. Drolma grasps it in both of hers. "You're a real piece of work, Drolma."

"And now I understand why Jake was such a wonderful man. He had such a wonderful father."

Jamie looks at Drolma, his face covered in worry. "What about my practice?"

Drolma puts her hands on Jamie's shoulders as she looks into his eyes. "What about it? It is *your* practice. Continue to do what you have been doing."

"What if I have a question? I can't exactly call you on your cell."

"Ah, *Dampa Garma Pawo*... you and I, we will only have to think of one another to be together. Just sit for a while, think about your question, and don't be surprised when the answer comes."

Angela turns to Drolma. "Look, Drolma... you can't just disappear from our lives. May we come to Ladakh to visit sometime?"

Drolma smiles, "I will be here. And you will come. We'll go for a walk in the mountains with the snow leopards." She looks at Jamie. "It's very beautiful there and don't worry. They tell me they like you!"

They watch the car pull up. Samten Rinpoche steps out, followed by Chökli Rinpoche carrying Jikme. Samten Rinpoche embraces each one of them. He playfully tugs on Ed's new beard and says, "So, things have a way of working out after all."

Chökli Rinpoche places Jikme on the ground, and the child immediately sees Ed, walks over, and stares up. He reaches out to be picked up. Ed squats down so they are eye-to-eye. He winks, "Hi."

The child reaches out and pats Ed's face, then nuzzles his cheek. Then he turns and stretches his arms up to Jamie. Jamie scoops him up. "Hey, Jikme... oof!... you're getting heavy!"

The child makes a tiny fist and begins an awkward bang/tap/grab. Jamie laughs, and finishes it for him. "You are such a cool little dude!"

Chökli Rinpoche retrieves Jikme, and hands him to Drolma. He whispers into Samten Rinpoche's ear, and Samten Rinpoche nods as he speaks. "There may be some who would look for us here. It would be best if we left right now." He holds the door open. "Please."

Angela, Ed and Jamie climb into the vehicle, as the two Rinpoches settle in. Samten Rinpoche motions to the driver and he immediately puts the car in gear and begins to drive away.

Jamie looks around. "Wait! Where's Jikme?"

Ed looks back over his shoulder. "What the... where'd they go?"

Angela and Jamie look around, and indeed, Drolma and Jikme are both gone, and then something catches Ed's eye. "How—?"

Drolma could not possibly have climbed the hundred-foot high, shear-faced hill so quickly but there she is, along with her two snow leopards and carrying Jikme. She stops to face down at them, smiles and waves. Jikme laughs and does his best to wave too.

Ed laughs as he waves back. "Cute kid. The way he patted my face and rubbed his cheek against mine; that's what Jake used to do when he… when…"

Angela is staring at Ed as he stumbles for words. She whispers, "Oh my God…" Angela and Ed both look out of the window, but Drolma and Jikme have disappeared.

Jamie shakes his head as he looks for them. "The guys at school would never believe me if I told them about her. She's a real-life superhero. This is such a cool place… we've got to come back." He looks at Ed, then Angela. "What is it?"

Angela hugs Jamie to hide her tears. "I'm just glad we're all safe together and going home."

Jamie looks at Ed, who is mightily trying to hide wiping his eyes. "Are you crying, Grandpa?"

"Hell no! It's all this dust up here."

Jamie falls back in the seat and his mouth opens in a huge yawn. "Man, all of a sudden I can't believe how tired I am." Almost immediately, his eyes close and he's deep asleep. Angela puts a jacket over the sleeping boy, then looks over at Samten Rinpoche.

"You knew all along."

The Rinpoche doesn't immediately answer. "His mother is here, and they'll stay with Drolma for some time. Because of circumstances, his training will begin much earlier than is usual."

Ed shakes his head. "I don't understand any of this."

Samten Rinpoche turns to Ed, "But you could. You'd only need to spend some time with us, if you were so inclined. And we have so much that needs to be done. I'm guessing that a man with your skills would be of great benefit and would be very busy here. You know that all of you are always most welcome."

Ed looks at the sleeping boy, then at Angela. "There's a lot we need to talk about."

Angela reaches over and takes Ed's hand. Rinpoche turns around, leans back in his seat and nods off as Angela and Ed look out of their windows, both lost in their thoughts.

DHARAMSALA

Jamie, Ed and Angela sit huddled around Jamie's computer in the darkened room. Jamie taps on the keys as he speaks, "I'll run it again."

They watch the screen as it shows the last images of 2014 BD recorded by EarthShield 4 as the asteroid begins to grow in size, just moments before the detonation of the thermonuclear device. The image freezes as part of it zooms larger. Dr. Johansson's disembodied voice emerges from the laptop's speaker:

"Now, see these luminous particles streaming into the asteroid? If the asteroid were expanding from gases heating internally, one would assume that the particles, whatever they are, should be moving outwardly. So, it appears that something from the outside is going inside the asteroid." He pauses for a long moment, as if trying to think of what next to say. *"We have absolutely no explanation for this observation. Not even a clue."*

The three of them sit for a long moment, silently staring at the screen, and then each other. Jamie breaks the silence as he nods.

"Drolma. She knows."

EPILOGUE

NEW YORK CITY, JUNE 12, THE FOLLOWING YEAR

The applause is deafening as the lights come up inside the darkened auditorium. Angela, standing in front of a set of huge photographs of Tibetan art, takes the microphone. She waits for her audience to settle and looks out over the hundreds of expensively dressed attendees, some wearing variations of Indian *saris*, Tibetan *chubas*, and lots of beads and *malas*. Their faces are attentive, concerned, as she begins to speak.

"You've just seen only a taste of what this precious culture has to offer the world. We need financial help and volunteers if it is to be preserved. The restoration and building of traditional schools and monasteries, the opening of clinics providing both western and eastern modalities of treatment, the creation of a system offering microloans for the establishment of small farms and other income producing enterprises... all of these things are only the beginning, and of course, we shouldn't exclude whatever political influence we can bring to this issue. Whatever you can do would be so greatly appreciated."

The audience stands and applauds as Angela brings her hands to her heart and bows her head.

LOS ANGELES

Slammer purposefully strides up the sidewalk toward the high school, eyes locked straight ahead as he works his way through the crowd of students, muttering a fleeting "sorry" or "'scuse me" as he brushes past the clumps of youths. There's an almost feral intensity in his eyes as he lasers in on one corner of the front steps of the structure, where Jamie stands to one side, phone up to his ear, "Grandpa... yeah... what?... you got the visas? Great! Yeah, I'll be home soon—"

Slammer's voice cuts through the air as he shouts, "Yo! Jamie!"

Jamie looks up from his phone to see Slammer leaping up the stairs, three at a time, straight for him. A few of the kids back away, faces suddenly fearful— Slammer's reputation is well known. Suddenly, Slammer's arms reach out as he grabs Jamie, hugging him close and spinning him around and around, laughing like a madman. He reaches into his jacket and pulls out a letter. "Read it!"

Jamie untangles himself, pushes Slammer away and catches his breath. "What is it? What happened?"

Slammer hands him the envelope. "Read it!"

Jamie looks at the envelope, then back up at Slammer. "This isn't your letter. It's addressed to some guy named Winston."

"Yeah, that's cute, smart guy. Go ahead 'n read it."

Jamie pulls the letter out and begins to read, "... and we are pleased to offer you a three-year apprenticeship at Barnard Industries, specializing in CNC manufacturing beginning September 8—"

"And dude... I got the scholarship. It's all paid for!"

Jamie laughs as he begins the tap/bang/grab fist thing and Slammer joins in. Slammer then grabs Jamie by the arms, and leans in, "Listen, man... I never would have got this thing without you. You got me ready, man, and you did it while doubling up your own classes. Never woulda' happened without you. I owe you big time, little bro'."

"Hey, I just showed you how. You did the work. I'm really happy for you. This is very cool."

Slammer steps back and takes a hard look at Jamie. He shakes his head, thinking... *this gotta be the whitest kid I ever met...* holds his hand up almost like a high-five, then grabs Jamie's hand and pulls it into his chest. "Slammer don't forget his friends. You ever need somethin'… someone… *anything,* you damn well better be callin' me first, you hear?"

"Yeah. I hear you."

Slammer smiles. "Good. Got that straight. Gotta go see Jackson now. Man, he ain't gonna believe this shit! Catch you later."

Jamie grins as he watches Slammer bound up the rest of the stairs and disappear into the school… *we look different… we act differently… but we really <u>are</u> all the same… and we all want the same things in the end…* as he absentmindedly runs his right thumb along the bottom of his left wrist, where, over the past several weeks and just above that place where, if the light is just right, the beating pulse of his heart is sometimes made visible, a newly emerging

has begun to appear. He glances down at it and smiles in anticipation.

ACKNOWLEDGEMENTS

(and a few confessions)

Just in case, so there's no misunderstanding, please remember that this is a work of fiction. It's a fantasy. As far as I know, there is no *Korlo Gön-Poy, Gönpoy-ri, Dampa Garma Pawo*; no Tibetan lineage of *Tokden-Ö-Zel*, etc., etc. I confess—I made these up. Now, there *may* be an asteroid out there with our name on it but please, whatever "visions" I might have had in putting this story together were, to the best of my knowledge, generated by my own sometimes overactive imagination.

"*Jamie's Rock*" began over a decade ago with a shower early one morning. As I was lathering up, I happened to visualize an asteroid slamming into the earth. For some reason, I found the violence of the imagery mesmerizing—it caused me to freeze in place for what seemed to be several minutes. Now, this was long before the release of several "disaster" movies that dealt with similar topics, but I had been reading about the NEAT (Near Earth Asteroid Tracking) program and I'm quite sure that's what provided the germ of this momentary fantasy. My next thought was... *what if this wasn't just a random case of cosmological bad luck... why would this happen?*

At the time, I was deeply involved in the study of Tibetan Buddhism, and its influence certainly colored almost everything in my life. I was also attempting to learn to read and write Tibetan with the help of my good friend David Curtis, a fellow Vietnam vet and classical linguist. He and his lovely wife Deanna, made the brilliant life choice of going through the training and the three year retreat required to become Tibetan Buddhist lamas. They founded and now administer the Tibetan Language Institute. (www.tibetanlanguage.org).

One thing led to another and over the course of a few weeks, I had the outlines of a story that first took form as a screenplay. Since I didn't know anyone in Hollywood who could "green-light" a movie, I put it on the shelf with a few other scripts and there it sat.

Late in 2011, one of my yoga pals and one of the loveliest, nicest people you'll ever meet, Kayoko Mitsumatsu (http://yogagivesback.org), introduced me to her equally splendid significant other, Ken Atchity (www.kenatchityblog.com). Ken is one of those courtly, well-educated Southern gentlemen, a writer himself and quite the chef. He took some time out of his busy schedule to sit down with me and asked about some of the stories I'd worked on. Much to my surprise, he suggested that I turn *"Jamie's Rock"* into a book.

"Really? *'Jamie's Rock'*? And a book?" I said disappointingly. I was hoping to pursue a screenplay, especially one about Afghanistan that I'd recently rewritten.

"Sure. Just write a few chapters and see how it goes."

I did, and he probably knew all along that I'd get sucked in and take it to the end. So, thank you Kayoko for the introduction and Ken, for giving me the push to attempt this novel.

I'm told every writer needs a good editor and now I'm truly a believer. About a year or so ago, I'd met Regina Hall where I practice Ashtanga yoga and been completely smitten. Regina is a very well known and respected actor, but, besides being gorgeous and simply one of the funniest women I've ever met, she has a sharp and incisive mind. She read a couple of my screenplays and offered some brilliant suggestions that I instantly and gratefully applied. Regina was there when the first draft of "Jamie's Rock" was done and enthusiastically waded through it to make her notes. When we sat down to go over them, it was as if night had become day—her suggestions were spot on regarding tone, story, timing and character. I think I incorporated everything she noted. Regina, I can't thank you enough for your kindness and for sharing that sharp mind of yours.

Turns out that my Ashtanga practice room had another treasure to share—China Adams. China is a marvelous artist, teaches art, and curates exhibitions (www.chinaadamsart.com). I asked China if she had any idea how I might go about creating a book cover. That was all I needed to say—she jumped in with both feet, but what was most interesting was that her first concept was *exactly* what I had visualized, even down to the coloration. Everyone I have shown her concept to thought it was beautifully executed. She has been an incredibly valuable resource, and an encouraging, generous and marvelous friend. Thank you, China, for all your assistance and patience.

Stanford Whitmore is a novelist and a screenwriter from the Hollywood of a number of years ago. Meeting Stan was the fortunate fallout of the unfortunate publicity regarding one of the supposedly "covert" activities I had been a part of years ago. Writing was only one of the common denominators— Stan was a gunner in a US Navy TBF torpedo bomber during WWII and we've swapped lots of "there I was" stories over the years. I'm sure he was a pretty good gunner, but when it comes to writing, Stan is a master. Every time I read anything he has written, I kick myself and mutter something like, "Damn, I wish I'd written that!" He is an artist, pure and simple. Stan once told me that "You can outline all you want but once you begin to write, the characters will lead you where they will. Most of the time it's where you need to go." He is so very right. Stan has always been generous with his time, suggestions, encouragement, and praise. Stan, you have been a major reason why I kept at this for so long. Many thanks to you and Sylvia, your very patient and understanding wife.

When I returned from Vietnam, I brought a little something home with me—an undiagnosed, raging case of PTSD. Some thirty years later, a definitive diagnoses helped to explain years of frustration, anger and what were to me, a mysterious propensity to seek out physically dangerous and often quixotic endeavors.

One of the major reasons that I'm still here banging away on this keyboard is because of my exposure and involvement in the Tibetan Buddhist teachings and practices. My introduction came after I read *"The Tibetan Book Of Living And Dying"* by Sogyal Rinpoche, one of the preeminent teachers of Tibetan Buddhism today (www.rigpa.org).

Even if you have absolutely no interest in Buddhism or Tibet, *"The Tibetan Book Of Living And Dying"* is a beautifully written, fascinating window into a relatively unknown world.

Tibetan Buddhism is the defining element of a fascinating culture that underwent a remarkable transformation that began with the arrival of a "basket of Buddhist scriptures" from India approximately fifteen-hundred years ago, and the appearance of Padmasambhava, the "Second Buddha", some seven-hundred plus years after that. To the uninformed, it can be wildly complex with its incredibly beautiful iconography, its many rituals and practices, and yet at its heart, the simple teachings of love and compassion are also at the core of so many of the world's religions.

The result was that Tibet's physical isolation and mountainous geography, coupled with its previous cultural history and the profound teachings of Buddhism, led to a synergy that created a "spiritual technology" producing some of the most spiritually advanced and simply amazing beings ever seen on this earth.

I've met many Tibetan Buddhist teachers over the years and it is a testament to the power of their spiritual accomplishment that in spite of the horrors that have been visited upon Tibet since 1950, the loss of their homeland, and the repression and torture of their people, I have never seen any of these teachers show any animus toward the Chinese people or nation. To the contrary, they welcome with open arms anyone interested in the teachings.

If the reader is interested in learning more about the conditions inside Tibet today, I can recommend no better source than Matteo Pistono's splendid book, *In the Shadow of the Buddha: One Man's Journey of Discovery.* (www.matteopistono.com). Matteo's book is the utterly fascinating story of his personal pilgrimage, and he provides many references for those who wish to know exactly the nature of the tragedy that is modern Tibet.

Everything I used that relates to Tibet or Buddhism was examined over and over again to insure that there would be no disrespect or perversion of the teachings.

Obviously, the elements of some teachings were included but hopefully, in a way that shows the great respect they deserve. I did take a few "technical" liberties but only when required to drive the story.

That leads to another confession regarding the mantra that plays such a central role, the one that appears on Jamie's body, on the prayer wheel, etc. Unknown to my friend David Curtis, I spent some long evenings with my Tibetan-English dictionary creating it (a splendid example of a little knowledge being a very dangerous thing). I didn't want to take anything that was actually used in the Tibetan Buddhist liturgy and risk misunderstanding by showing it used improperly.

"Jamie's Rock" is in the main a work of fiction, and all errors or mistakes found in this work were totally unintentional and mine alone. Should the reader take issue with anything they find in these writings, please accept my profound apology—it was not my intention to offend.

This is a time of great peril for Tibet. It is my hope and prayer that one of the world's greatest treasures, the people and the wisdom culture of Tibet, survive and prosper in the coming years for the benefit of all.

It is because of them that I am reminded daily of the interconnectedness of everyone and everything, that harm done to one is done to all, and that we really are all in this together.

Thanks, and my very best wishes.

Gary Goldman
Los Angeles,
December 16, 2012

www.ingramcontent.com/pod-product-compliance
Lightning Source LLC
Chambersburg PA
CBHW070317260626
47160CB00003B/870